To Simon !

The LOXLEYS and the WAR of 1812

Writer
Alan Grant

Illustrator
Claude St. Aubin

Colourist
Lovern Kindzierski

Letters
Todd Klein

War of 1812 Summary by
Mark Zuehlke

Editor
Alexander Finbow

RENEGADE
ARTS ENTERTAINMENT

Published by Renegade Arts Canmore Ltd trading as Renegade Arts Entertainment Ltd
Office of publication: 30 Prospect Heights, Canmore, Alberta T1W 2S8 Canada

Renegade Arts Entertainment is
Alexander Finbow   Alan Grant   Doug Bradley
John Finbow   Nick Wilson and Jennifer Taylor.

Scan this QR code to visit our War of 1812 website:

www.renegadeartsentertainment.com

ISBN: 978-0-9868200-0-7

First Printing April 2012

Graphic Novel written by Alan Grant
Illustrated by Claude St. Aubin
Colours by Lovern Kindzierski
Letters, logo and cover design by Todd Klein
War of 1812 Historical Summary written by Mark Zuehlke
Editor and publisher Alexander Finbow

Printed in Canada by Friesens

Major General Isaac Brock

CONTENTS

FOREWORD

'Why create a graphic novel set during the War of 1812?'

That's a question I have been asked many times over the 3 years it took to put this book together. The simple answer is that I had an opportunity to tell a story that should be told and hadn't been told using a comic book approach before, at the perfect moment in time for the 200th anniversary of this little known and often misunderstood conflict approached.

I hadn't even heard of this war that involved my country of birth, England, my new home, Canada, and the world's current superpower that is not usually shy about military history. Despite studying history at high school, my introduction to the War of 1812 came in The Hudson's Bay store in Banff whilst killing time at the hands of a copy of AMAZING STORIES 'The War of 1812 Against The States', as my wife Karen tried on clothes.

Up until then 1812 meant Napoleon, France and Wellington, I had never heard mention of it in England or Canada before. How could a conflict which defined the future of a continent, included burning down the White House and present day Toronto, and also involved the American indigenous people's strongest coordinated resistance to extermination, have been so neglected for so long?

Renegade was established to tell great stories and here was a great story ready to be told. With one of the greatest comic book writers, Alan Grant, also a founder member of our creative little company, I knew if we could work out the right approach to the story that he would deliver a compelling and involving narrative, and Alan did. The Loxleys give us the human connection to the politics and conflict of the time.

Next up, Claude and Lovern accepted the artistic challenge of realising our story in a style that would attract new readers to a medium they might otherwise have ignored since their childhood, and existing comic book readers would appreciate equally.

I'm happy to say the artwork from both has exceeded my expectations. Todd Klein was our first choice letterer and happily for us he was keen to be involved too. Once the comic book production was underway I approached Mark Zuehlke, whose book *For Honours Sake - The War of 1812*, I'd found to be very involving and even handed in chronicling the events of the war. Mark's mission was to create a summary of the war for the second half of our book for the reader who enjoyed the comic strip and wanted to know more about the history straight away.

Somewhere along the way I decided it would be a great idea to adapt the book into a school play for Canadian students to really get involved in their history with. Enter Tab Murphy, stage right. An Oscar nominated Hollywood screenwriter living just the other side of our small mountain town and happy to jump onboard our intriguing project.

Tab was the second American to join our very Canadian venture, but he embraced the challenge and has written a wonderful school play that should be performed in schools long after the bicentenary has passed. In fact, our local middle school that my daughters attend is in rehearsals to be the first school in Canada to perform the play. Hats off to Sonja Howatt for being the first teacher to take the plunge.

Whilst all this was taking place, I'd presented our web designer, Phil Linnell, with a timeline of the events of the war to build into an interactive online website to act as a hub for people wanting to quickly follow the historical events and also the planned bicentenary events. Phil succeeded in creating an easy to use and graphically pleasing online experience at www.1812timeline.com that has proved to be a great tool for students and history buffs alike.

Now, with the snow falling outside our mountain studio, the only piece of our 1812 puzzle left to finish is this foreword. My final words before you lose yourself in the rich world Alan and company have created, are that I sincerely hope you enjoy this journey into the past and its parallels with our modern world that are still as valid now as 200 years ago.

Alexander Finbow
March 7th 2012

ACKNOWLEDGEMENTS

Alexander Finbow

Many thanks to our creative team Alan, Mark, Claude, Lovern and Todd, for crafting my ideas into this wonderful book, and for their continued advice and help in making it happen. To my mother and father for their unwavering support. Karen, Leia and Phoebe for their invaluable help and love on this journey into the past.

Claude St. Aubin

I am extremely grateful to my wonderful best friend, my wife, for her support, help, patience and understanding of my very demanding career as a free-lance artist. My sincere thanks to Alexander Finbow for allowing me to play a part in the War of 1812 project. I was fortunate to be part of a wonderful and creative team and will always cherish this incredible opportunity.

Lovern Kindzierski

Would like to thank Chris Chuckry and Peter Dawes for their talented and timely assistance.

The LOXLEYS and the WAR of 1812

Alan Grant: writer
Claude St. Aubin: artist
Lovern Kindzierski: colours
Todd Klein: letters

FROM THE JOURNAL OF AURORA LOXLEY, FALL, 1811.

The harvest is in, and — praise the Lord! — it is a good one.

We have corn to take to the grinding mill in Queenston, and the vegetable patches have proved to be a cornucopia. A fine crop of apples means I will be kept busy for weeks, making us pickles and preserves to tide us through the winter.

It is true to say I never miss our old home in Pennsylvania, although not a day passes but I wish Abraham was still alive.

Washington Guardian

Volume IIL

THURSDAY, June 18, 1812

ber 35

ndian Raids Continue

...ilies trying to forge an honest ...ng along our western frontier find ...mselves the victims of marauding ...nds of Indians. Attacking these so ...punity and ... nothing of ...led war ... ...rning d ...tacking w ...gard for ...eaders wil ...not a n ...attacks be ...ormation

As we ... James R ... warning ... Canoe's ... the Hols ... received ... McDona ... for a c ... Hamilto ... Detroit, ... equivale ... packho ... respons ... assault ... Montg ... Tennes ... they ... elever ... Chick ... food ... home ... destr ... the ... Hols ... In th ... John ... Che ... atta ... so t ... dea ... Up ... tov ... th...

returned to Chickamaug ... vicinity. The Shawnee sent envoys to Chickamauga to find out if the destruction had caused Dragging Canoe's people to lose the will to fight, along with a sizable detachment of warriors to assist them in the South. In response to their inquiries, Dragging Canoe held up the war belts he accepted when the delegation visited Chota in 1776, and said, "We are not yet conquered". To cement the alliance, the Cherokee responded to the Shawnee gesture with nearly a hundred of their warriors sent to the North.

Th... w...

McDon... area for a co... Governor Hamilton was planning to hold at Detroit, and that a stockpile of supplies equivalent to that of a hundred packhorses was stored there. In response, he ordered a preemptive assault under Evan Shelby and John Montgomery. Boating down the Tennessee in a fleet of dugout canoes, they disembarked and destroyed the eleven towns in the immediate Chickamauga area and most of their food supply, along with McDonald's home and store. Whatever was not destroyed was confiscated and sold at the point where the trail back to the Holston crossed.

In the meantime, Dragging Canoe and John McDonald were leading the Cherokee and fifty Loyalist Rangers in attacks on Georgia and South Carolina, ...e resistance and only four

AMERICA GOES TO WAR!

Today in Washington during an address to Congress, President Madison made clear his intentions toward our former opponent Gre... extensi... borde...

...the balance, ...ops, poorly ...ll managed to ...eneralship of ...and his

...a differe... ...arm... ...n 17... ...s the great co... ...ng lived through ...confident in our ...clearly sure that ...al there can only ...e that will bring ...nation.

...he north is a long ...ose that plans are ...through to make ...ure as may be in ...in circumstances. ...order areas are no ...arming for the ...will be coming their ...ner, unless Britain ...ch different course

IMPENDING WAR

...ppers took advantage ...in Europe to absorb ...between Europe and ...panish islands in the ...breaking the passage ...US port, they evaded ...with a st... ...seizure u... ...which fo... ...trade ... ...peaceti... ...Essex C... ...U.S. sh... ...Americ... ...prohibi... ...As a r... ...ships b...

The ... ...institu...

Act of 1807. Difficulty of enforcement and economic conditions that rendered England and the Continent more or less independent o... ...the embargo ineffe... ...ay to a Non... ...was supe... ...which ...ons ag... ...e pro... ...ew its ...s, nor... ...reimposed wi...

In 1809, a... Noninterco... agreement b... British min... Erskine, wh...

...dubious co... James M... Jefferson ... (1811) n... Negotiati... the order... result; ju... war, yet... orders in...

At fi... with po... rather t... Preside... series ... Decem... These ... Americ... eventu... with ... possess...

Because the legislation failed to British policy and seriously harmed the U.S. economy as well, it was replaced by the Non-Intercourse Act in March 1809. This measure forbade trade with European belligerents until it was replaced in May 1810 by Macon's Bill ... ...opened American ...bject to the ...t of either ...repealing its ...United States ...nonintercourse ...ion failed to ...the remaining

...eon announced ...erlin and Milan ...anding that the ...also force Great ...neutral rights. ...ccepted this as ...icy had changed, ...810 he imposed ...st Great Britain. ...he repeal of the ...condition for the ...o American trade. ...refused to comply, ...11, summoned ...to an early session ...pare for war. After ...debate, Congress ...esident's initiatives ...18 June 1812. The ...y controversial ... ...Republican Party ...In the House of ...he vote was 79 to 49 ...enate, 19 to 3. The ...hose constituents ...y England) depended ...with Great Britain, ...France had equally ...American neutrality, ...he declaration of war ...s prosecution.

And thus we can see that all these events have been boiling and brewing in the background in both countries.

...embargo on trade... economic pressure would force the belligerents to negotiate with the United States. The Nonimportation Act of 1806 was followed by the Embargo.

Tecumseh campaign falters

Rumors of Tecumseh returning to the South last November have been confirmed. Hoping to gain the support of the southern tribes for his crusade to ...i... back our pioneering settlers. The ...Washington ...panied by ... Shawnee, ...d Sioux. ...the towns ...and Lower ...action, the ... Muscogee, ...g a sizable ...warriors, the ...an, The Big ...d Tecumseh

...tion from the ...t visited his ...atchee, that ...s to visit the ...idge, a warrior ...ber of the ...old him if he ...herokee Nation ...m). However, ...the South, he ...an enthusiastic ...and 19 Choctaw, ...north when he

...UROPE

...ar on our shores ...h deal with thi... ...they are alread... ...war with France ...s play out wi... ...Treaty of Tils... ...originally led to t... ...ar. With Fran... ...conquer or ally w... ...n had to be seen ...be able to support and defend its o... European partners. British Men-of-... supported the Swedish fleet during ... Finish War and had victories over ... Russians in the Gulf of Finland in ... 1808 and August 1809. However, ... success of the Russian army on ... land forced Sweden to ... peace-treaties with Russia in 1809 ... with France in 1810 and to join ... Continental Blockade against B... But Franco-Russian relations be... progressively worse after 1810, an... Russian war with the British effe... ended. In April 1812, Britain, ... and Sweden signed secret agree... directed against Napoleon. Na... had enjoyed easy success in ... retaking Madrid, defeating the ... and consequently forcing a wit... of the heavily out-numbered ... army from the Iberian Peninsul... 16th January 1809). But when ... the guerilla war against his ... the countryside continued to ... great numbers of troops. ... attack prevented Napoleo... successfully wrapping up o... against British forces by nec... his departure for Austria, and ... returned to the Peninsula thea... absence and that of his best ... (Davout remained in ... throughout the war) th... situation in Spain deterio... then became dire when ... Wellesley arrived to take ... British-Portuguese forces. ... Masséna returned toward ... relieve Almeida; Wellingto... checked the French at th... Fuentes do Onoro. Sir... Viscount Beresford fought ... of the South' to a m... standstill at the Battle of ... May, Wellington was pro... General for his services. ... abandoned Almeida, s... from British pursuit, bu...

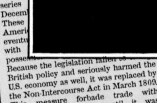

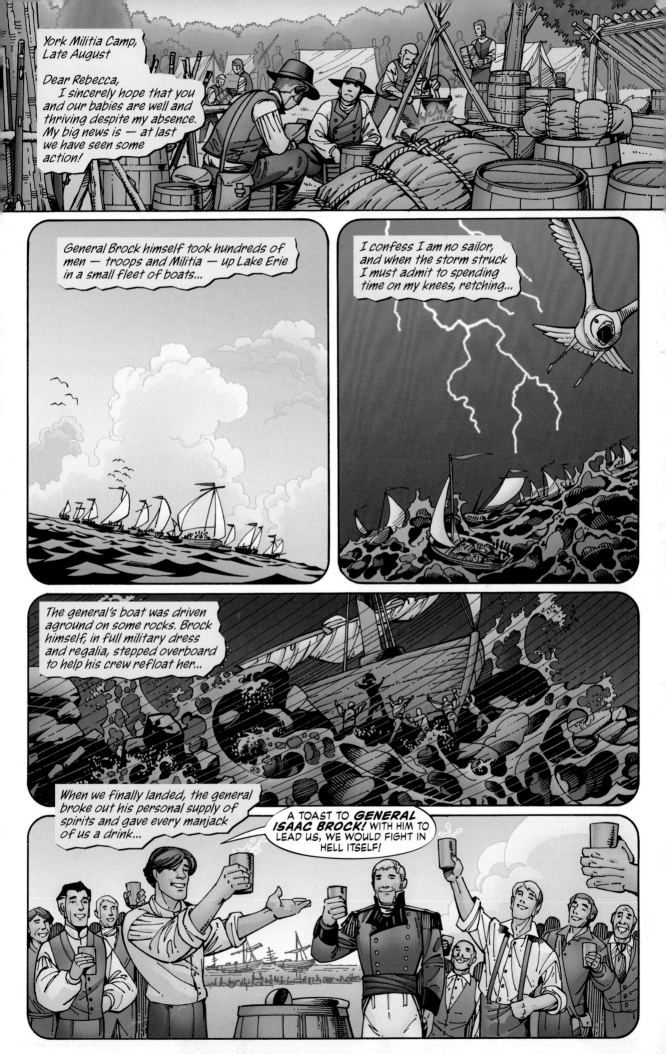

Brock and Tecumseh greeted each other like old friends. Both are tall and powerful men, and natural leaders.

Just seeing them keeps a man's spirits from sinking low!

Even with the Indians, our forces were vastly outnumbered. In an attempt to intimidate the Americans, the general paraded his troops just out of gunshot range...

SIR! IT IS TOO DANGEROUS FOR YOU TO EXPOSE YOURSELF!

He made the Militia share uniforms with the troopers, so it looked as if there were twice as many regular troops...

I WOULD NEVER ASK MY MEN TO GO WHERE I AM NOT WILLING TO LEAD THEM.

Then he had Tecumseh march his warriors past the fort three or four times. It must have seemed to them the entire Indian nation was turned out for battle...

GENERAL BROCK'S COFFIN WAS CARRIED FROM **NEWARK** TO **FORT GEORGE**, FOLLOWED BY THAT OF HIS TRUSTED AIDE, MacDONELL. THOUSANDS OF CITIZENS LINED THE ROUTE, OFFERING THEIR GRATITUDE AND PRAYERS.

BROCK GAVE THE CANADAS HIS **COURAGE**, HIS **LOYALTY**, AND ULTIMATELY HIS **LIFE**.

PERHAPS MOST IMPORTANTLY, HE GAVE CANADIANS **CONFIDENCE** IN THEMSELVES AND THEIR ABILITIES.

IT WAS THE **FUNERAL** OF A **GENERAL**...AND THE BIRTH OF A **LEGEND**.

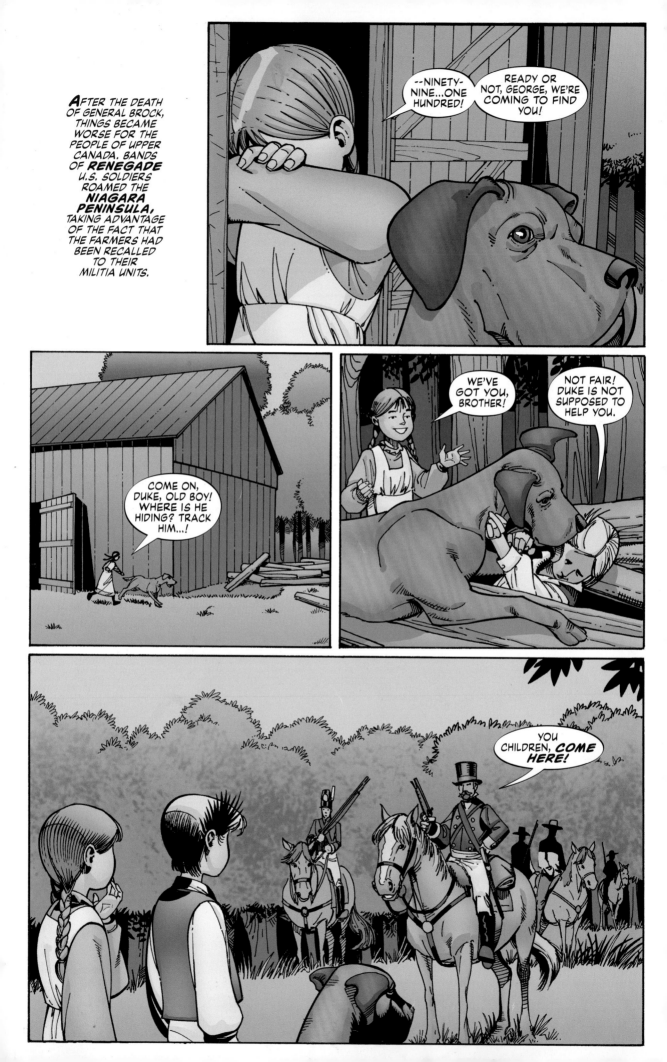

Dear Ma,
I am so sorry for doing this, but I can see no other way forward. The Americans have killed my beloved grandmother, and shot my faithful dog. I must find some way to hit back at them. So I have left home, and will seek out Pa and Matthew at their barracks in York.

Do not worry about me— I will keep off the tracks, and remain hidden from any renegades. Please forgive me.

TOO STEEP FOR ME TO CLIMB DOWN.

Your loving son, George.

THIS WILL PROVE AN EASIER CROSSING POINT...

HELP! HELP!

HELP!

York Militia Camp, November, 1812

Dearest Rebecca,
Something happened today which will make you—and perhaps one day our daughters—proud of me. In an attempt to contain the lawless U.S. renegades, Lt. James Fitzgibbon has handpicked and trained a special force to combat them. They are called the Green Tigers...and I have been selected to be one of their number! Your loving husband,
Matthew

CUT HIM DOWN!

SOME OF YOU OTHERS-- PUT OUT THOSE FLAMES.

WHO HAS VISITED THIS EVIL UPON YOU?

A-AMERICANS! WHEN MY HUSBAND TRIED TO STAND UP TO THEM, THEY BEAT HIM FIERCELY, AND THEN-- THEN--

THEY STOLE ALL OUR SUPPLIES, AND SET FIRE TO THE HOUSE. THEY SAID IT WOULD BE A LESSON FOR OTHERS NOT TO RESIST.

ANDREW-- DAVID. SALVAGE WHAT YOU CAN FROM THE HOUSE AND AFTERWARD DELIVER THESE PEOPLE TO THEIR NEIGHBOURS.

PARDON MY ASKING--BUT WILL WE BE SAFE...?

WE COME IN PEACE. THEY WILL RECEIVE US IN PEACE.

WHAT AMUSES THEM SO?

THE *PALENESS* OF YOUR SKIN. THEY ASK IF IT DOES NOT REFLECT THE SUNSHINE, LIKE A MIRROR.

THE NEWS IS NOT SO GOOD. WHILE WE HAVE BEEN HEADED NORTH AND EAST, TECUMSEH HAS GONE SOUTH.

HE SEEKS TO CONVINCE THE TRIBES THERE TO *JOIN* HIS FIGHT AGAINST AMERICA.

THE SKY IS CLEAR. THE NORTH WIND IS CHILL. THEY SAY THIS MEANS A HARD WINTER WILL COME.

THE WOMEN AND CHILDREN GO TO THE FORT AT NIAGARA. THE BRITISH WILL HELP THEM WITH FOOD.

NEITHER SIDE HAD A MONOPOLY ON ATROCITIES. ON JANUARY 19, 1813, LT. COLONEL PROCTOR AND HIS ARMY CROSSED THE FROZEN **DETROIT RIVER.**

WITH THE AID OF WYANDOT **CHIEF ROUNDHEAD** AND HIS WARRIORS, THEY ATTACKED RIVER RAISIN AND WON IT BACK FROM THE AMERICANS WHO OCCUPIED IT.

500 PRISONERS WERE TAKEN, AND LEFT IN THE CARE OF THE INDIANS, WHO HAD LOOTED THE VILLAGES LIQUOR SUPPLY.

FOR THE REST OF THE WAR, U.S. TROOPS WOULD RALLY TO THE BATTLE-CALL: *"REMEMBER RIVER RAISIN!"*

Montreal, Almost Spring, 1813

Ellen, ma chère femme—

The long winter is nearly over, and my heart pines for you more each day.

It seems the Americans thought that the French-Canadians would rise up and join them in their fight against England. But as is often the way of it, we French acted totally contrary to expectations.

I have been placed under the command of Lt. Col. Charles-Michel d'Irumberry de Salaberry, a remarkable name for a most remarkable man. I have trained with his special forces unit, the Voltigeurs.

FitzGibbon was astonished to see the frail, disheveled figure--

--but he acted on her news at once.

AWAKEN THE MEN. SHORE UP OUR DEFENCES--AND SEND FOR **REINFORCEMENTS** AT ONCE!

WHEN BATTLE CAME, IT WAS NATIVE INDIANS WHO LED THE ATTACK. AS MANY AS A HUNDRED AMERICANS DIED BEFORE THEIR COMMANDER SURRENDERED.

AS INDIAN LEADER **JOHN NORTON** LATER REMARKED, "THE **COGNAWAGA** INDIANS FOUGHT THE BATTLE, THE **MOHAWKS** GOT THE PLUNDER, AND **FITZGIBBON** GOT THE CREDIT."

IT WOULD BE MANY YEARS BEFORE LAURA SECORD'S PART IN THE VICTORY WAS ACCEPTED, AND EVEN LONGER BEFORE SHE WAS REWARDED FOR HER UNFLINCHING BRAVERY.

It was our happiest day since he left us.

YOU LOOK STRONG AND FIT, LITTLE BROTHER.

AND YET... I SEE GREAT SORROW IN YOUR EYES.

THERE, DO NOT CRY. YOU ARE HOME NOW.

And then he told his heartbreaking tale...

PROCTOR HALTED THE RETREAT AT MORAVIAN TOWN. THE TROOPS WERE HUNGRY, AND AMMUNITION WAS LOW.

MANY OF TECUMSEH'S WARRIORS HAD ABANDONED HIM, BELIEVING OUR FORCES WERE DESTINED FOR DEFEAT.

"FIREBRAND AND I WERE EAGER TO SEE OUR FIRST ACTION. WITHOUT ASKING, WE JOINED TECUMSEH'S WARRIORS WHERE THEY WAITED BY A SWAMP...

Newark
December, 1813

My dearest Eliza,

Prepare for a shock. I am afraid this missive contains some very bad news, not only about the war but also about my own personal circumstances.

My Militia unit had been placed under the command of that well-known soldier, William Hamilton Merritt.

Also fighting with us was a detachment of American slaves who had escaped to the Canadas...

We ambushed a party of enemy soldiers close to 40-mile Creek.

On this occasion, Fortune was not with me...

AAGH!

Had it not been for two of the escapees, I might have been taken prisoner—or, worse, executed where I fell.

I had been shot twice, in the elbow and shoulder of my left arm. My saviours took me to a British field hospital.

With no medication available, the surgeon had no choice...

I WILL HAVE TO *AMPUTATE.*

I was sent to Newark to recuperate, where an elderly couple—John and Agnes Muirhead—kindly took me in.

On the eve of the 10th, the Hell-spawned traitor Joseph Willcocks and his men rode into the frozen town...

TEN DAYS LATER, FIRED BY A FURIOUS DESIRE FOR REVENGE, MERRITT'S DRAGOONS CROSSED THE NIAGARA RIVER...

...AND LAID WASTE TO THE AMERICAN FORT THERE. BUT THAT WAS ONLY THE **START** OF THE REPRISALS.

LAKE ONTARIO

Ft. MISSISSAUGA

NEWARK
Ft. GEORGE

Ft. NIAGARA
YOUNGSTON

N

WITHIN DAYS, THE ENTIRE AMERICAN FRONTIER FROM **FORT NIAGARA** TO **BUFFALO** WAS PUT TO THE TORCH.

NEW YORK

St DAVIDS
QUEENSTON

LEWISTON

STAMFORD

DEVIL'S HOLE

LUNDY'S LANE

MANCHESTER
Ft. SCHLOSSER

NIAGARA FALLS
CHIPPEWA

OAK BLUFF

CANADA

MORE THAN ANY OTHER ATROCITY, THE DESTRUCTION OF NEWARK FUSED THE BRITISH, THE MILITIA AND THE CIVILIANS INTO ONE UNITED MASS. ONLY THE WINTER'S FIERCE COLD PREVENTED FURTHER RECRIMINATION.

BLACK ROCK

Ft. ERIE

BUFFALO

LAKE ERIE

WITH THE ADVENT OF THE SPRING THAW, THE MILITIA WAS RECALLED AS THE NIAGARA PENINSULA AGAIN CAME UNDER U.S. ATTACK.

TIRED OF BETRAYAL BY AMERICAN SPIES AND SYMPATHISERS, THE GOVERNMENT ARRESTED A NUMBER OF SUSPECTED **TRAITORS.** AFTER TRIAL, SEVERAL WERE HANGED AT **BURLINGTON HEIGHTS.**

JOSEPH WILLCOCKS' RAIDERS CONTINUED THEIR DEADLY ASSAULTS, BURNING VILLAGES AND FARMS. HUNDREDS OF SETTLERS FLED TO THE FORTS AFTER THEIR LIVESTOCK AND SUPPLIES WERE STOLEN.

EARLY IN JULY, A LARGE AMERICAN FORCE CAPTURED **FORT ERIE,** THEN MARCHED ON **CHIPPEWA,** WHERE THEY INFLICTED A CRUSHING DEFEAT ON BRITISH AND CANADIAN TROOPS.

FROM THE JOURNAL OF AURORA LOXLEY.

July, 1814

After much painful contemplation, Aaron and I have decided that— in face of the dangers—we have no option but to leave our home.

We have joined with many others heading for the safety of the British forts. We have taken everything of value we can carry, and all of our livestock.

But we have left our hearts behind, in this homestead we love so much...

It is especially hard for Ellen, for now she is with child, and we have heard that Pierre's Voltigeurs are engaged in fighting in Lower Canada.

I feel as if this is happening in a dream, or rather, a nightmare. Who knows if we will ever see our home again?

I am weary to my very bones, and feel like the Indians must feel, when the Americans drive them off their land and onto Reservations.

Many times has my faith been badly shaken. But I am sure the Good Lord will see us through in the end.

Only one good thing has come out of the disruption. Verity and George have met others of their own age; perhaps it will help George recover from his grief at FireBrand's tragic end.

And Verity is just starting to realise that she is, in fact, an attractive young lady.

The twins, meanwhile, have discovered that other living, breathing, real children actually exist!

Aurora used to counsel us to always look for the good when something untoward interfered in our lives. So, even in the midst of death and disruption, I try to appreciate the happiness of our children.

A small blessing, like a candle glowing in a sea of darkness.

July 30, 1814

My dear wife 'Becca—

One week ago, we fought the hardest, most bloody battle it has been my misfortune to participate in. It took place at Lundy's Lane...

Despite the numerical superiority of our troops, the enemy fought like demons. The battle roared on all afternoon and deep into the night.

By morning, both sides were too exhausted to fight on. The Americans fled the field, but neither the Militia nor the British regulars were able to pursue them.

In all, almost a thousand men lost their lives.

We buried our fallen in a mass grave—

LORD, ACCEPT THE SOULS OF THESE BRAVE WARRIORS...

—but we were in no mind to afford the niceties to the enemy. The American dead were burned on a huge funeral pyre.

The war in Europe is over. Britain has won, they say, and will soon send new armies to help us. Each night I pray this madness will soon be over.

Each morning, I wake to find it never is.

My love goes to you and my family. I would give all the treasure in King George's realm to be with you now, and trust that one day soon, I shall be.

Your loving husband.

ON AUGUST 13TH, BRITISH AND CANADIAN FORCES LAID SIEGE TO THE CAPTURED FORT ERIE.

WHEN THE TRAITOR JOSEPH WILLCOCKS PERISHED IN THE LONG FIGHT, THEY SAY A *CHEER* WENT UP THROUGH ALL THE CANADAS.

DESPITE SUCCESSFULLY HOLDING THE FORT FROM OUR FORCES, IT WOULD NOT BE LONG BEFORE THE AMERICANS WITHDREW ENTIRELY FROM THE PENINSULA. THIS TIME, THEY WOULD NOT RETURN.

FROM THE JOURNAL OF AURORA LOXLEY.

Late September, 1814

The authorities say the Americans have gone, retreated to their own string of forts on their side of the river. They have lost no territory, they have gained no territory.

We were allowed to return home, escorted by British troopers. Almost everywhere was desolation. Houses had been looted, orchards cut down, fields overgrown with weeds.

And our homestead had not escaped.

I felt like opening my mouth wide, and unleashing a scream that would encapsulate all of my fears and frustrations since this pointless war began.

Vice-Admiral Gambier, legal expert William Adams and War Office official Henry Goulburn represented the King.

NOW THE WAR WITH NAPOLEON IS OVER, HIS MAJESTY BELIEVES OUR POLICY OF *IMPRESSMENT* IS NO LONGER NECESSARY...

The American negotiators included Albert Gallatin, Jonathan Russell, John Quincy Adams...

...and Henry Clay.

--FOR OUR PART, WE DECLARE A RETURN TO THE *BORDERS* THAT PREVAILED PRIOR TO 1812--

The same Henry Clay who had done everything in his power to <u>start</u> the war.

Our aim was to rebuild the home we loved...

...a home that had been destroyed by the manoeuvrings of the very men who now seemed pledged to peace.

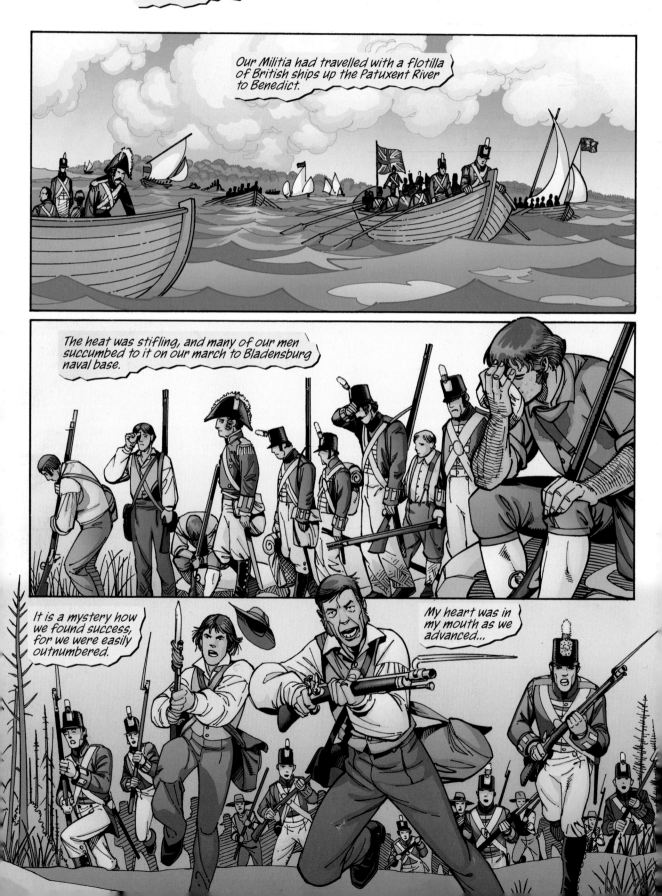

York Militia Camp
September

Dear 'Becca (and Ma and Pa and all the family),

You will never guess what I did last week. For a long time now, people have been talking about seeking revenge for the Americans' cowardly attack on York and our parliament. Well, on August 15, we finally achieved it!

Our Militia had travelled with a flotilla of British ships up the Patuxent River to Benedict.

The heat was stifling, and many of our men succumbed to it on our march to Bladensburg naval base.

It is a mystery how we found success, for we were easily outnumbered.

My heart was in my mouth as we advanced...

THE BRITISH AND CANADIANS SOUGHT TO KEEP UP THE MOMENTUM OF THEIR AGGRESSIVE CAMPAIGN. IN SEPTEMBER, **GOVERNOR PREVOST** LED 10,000 MEN INTO AMERICA...

...BUT HIS INSISTENCE ON PREMATURELY SENDING THE BRITISH WARSHIPS INTO ACTION ON **LAKE CHAMPLAIN** LED TO THEIR DEFEAT AT THE HANDS OF THE U.S. NAVY.

PREVOST'S NERVE FAILED WHEN HE SAW THE WRECKED AND CAPTURED SHIPS. HE TURNED TAIL, AND LED HIS ARMY HOME AGAIN.

THE PEACE HAD BEEN SIGNED WEEKS BEFORE NEW ORLEANS, BUT THE FRIGATES THAT CARRIED THE NEWS ACROSS THE OCEANS COULD TAKE UP TO **TWO MONTHS.**

MORE THAN **5,000** BRITISH SOLDIERS HAD BEEN **KILLED** OR **WOUNDED.** FOR THE UNITED STATES, THE FIGURE WAS **7,000.**

NO-ONE KNOWS HOW MANY **CANADIAN MILITIAMEN** DIED IN THE CAMPAIGN, OR HOW MANY **NATIVE INDIANS** GAVE THEIR LIVES IN PURSUIT OF TECUMSEH'S DREAM.

PERHAPS UNSURPRISINGLY, THE **INDIANS** CAME OFF WORST. THE U.S. CONTINUED ITS EXPANSIONIST POLICIES, STEADILY CONFINING THE NATIVES TO SMALLER AND SMALLER PARCELS OF LAND.

ALTHOUGH THE INDIANS HAD LIVED IN HARMONY WITH THEIR LAND FOR **TWENTY THOUSAND YEARS,** UNLESS THEY AGREED TO SETTLE AND FARM EUROPEAN-STYLE, THEY WERE TREATED AS PRIMITIVE SAVAGES WITH NO RIGHTS.

WITH TECUMSEH GONE, THEIR HEARTS WERE BROKEN.

FROM THE JOURNAL OF AURORA LOXLEY, APRIL, 1815.

At long last, our prayers were answered, the war ended, and our borders are safe again. Much remained the same, but more had been irrevocably changed.

Flora and Dahlia are growing up at what seems a prodigious rate. They are such a happy family, despite the fact Matthew still suffers nightmares from the horrors he has witnessed.

Irony of ironies: Pierre and Ellen's baby was born on the very day the peace was signed. Ellen has called him Pierre Isaac Brock Loxley, and he has become her whole life.

Aaron has adapted as best he can, and to see him swing his woodsman's axe one-handed is a minor miracle in itself.

Sometimes, in the evenings, I sit by candlelight and study the drawings William has made of our family.

I am often tormented by the losses we have suffered, but I try not to dwell on them. Whatever pain and misery we have endured, life must go on.

The future of the Canadas belongs to our children, and as Aurora always said: "For their sake, we must be brave."

The End

The War of 1812

Historical Summary

By Mark Zuehlke

THE OUTRAGES

If not for Henry Clay, the War of 1812 might never have happened. Many Americans fumed about the so-called "British outrages." When talk turned to going to war over them though, most people hesitated. President James Madison certainly did. He realized the United States was unprepared for war. There was no real army. It numbered barely 6,750 officers and enlisted men. States could raise militias, but the constitution forbade forcing militiamen to fight outside the country's borders. The navy existed more in name than substance. Fit for service were five frigates, three sloops, seven brigs, and sixty-two gunboats good only for coastal defense. Another five frigates listed alarmingly in various harbours awaiting vital repairs. Only 4,000 sailors and 1,800 marines served all these vessels.

Such a lack of readiness would give most sane men pause, but Clay was a man of ideas. Details were what others made happen. The thirty-five-year-old congressman had ridden into Washington thirsting for war. This would be a just and righteous war, Clay told all who would listen - and many did. How could they not? On November 4, 1811 the Kentucky congressman was elected Speaker of the House of Representatives in an unheard of two-to-one first-ballot vote.

Henry Clay

Next to President Madison, Clay was America's most powerful politician. He was also charismatic. At six feet, he towered over most people. He was roughly handsome; hair so blond it was almost white, blue eyes that varying light altered from pale to grey to robin's egg blue.

Clay looked like a leader, but it was his oratory that made him one. When the debates began on the very day that Clay stunned Congress by gliding effortlessly into the Speaker's chair, he used the power it invested to advance the cause of war.

Clay identified the "outrages" clearly. Impressment was the one guaranteed to most raise American ire, so it was impressment that Clay thunderously decried. Throughout the 1600s and 1700s, the Royal Navy had forced men to serve on its ships during times of war. In the early 1800s, Britain was again at war with Napoleon's France. The press gangs—hence the term impressment—scoured the streets of Britain in search of men to force into naval service. But the press gangs also struck wherever British ships entered harbours. Woe betide any man stopped on a foreign street who appeared British and could not prove different citizenship. Press-ganged he would be.

Such was the Royal Navy's thirst for men that merchant ships from other nations were routinely stopped on the high seas and searched for British subjects who could be pressed. Such a search often yielded good results, especially if the ship detained was American. Life on a Royal Navy ship was hard, so hundreds of impressed men deserted first chance they got. The United States was an obvious refuge. English was the common language. It was accepted that men were free and able to make of themselves what they would. A deserter who knew his way around ships could go to sea on an American merchant vessel and prosper. At least until it was waylaid by the Royal Navy and the press gangs came aboard.

Though America had won independence from Britain in 1783, few Britons accepted the notion of American citizenship. This was especially true of Royal Navy admirals. Before the revolution, those who now called themselves Americans had been subjects of the British Crown. Now the United States claimed that anyone residing inside its borders for a scant five years was American and could no longer be considered a British subject. It was a thin shield behind which many a man aboard an American merchant hid without success.

Clay claimed that as many as 50,000 legitimate Americans were impressed. Other American reports set the figure at 10,000. The numbers hardly mattered. Impressment was an affront to the authority of a young nation.

THE LEOPARD AFFAIR

The Leopard attacks the Chesapeake

Impressment of Americans began almost immediately after independence. While the practice angered the young nation, the federal government could do little more than cry foul. Regular complaints by America's ambassador fell on deaf ears in London. Then, on June 22, 1807, the impressment issue was raised to a new level of controversy. In the early hours, the Chesapeake ventured into international waters beyond Hampton Roads. Lurking close by was Leopard, a 50-gun ship of the line, whose captain knew that the smaller American frigate had British deserters aboard. The American captain denied that deserters were on Chesapeake and refused to be searched. Leopard attacked. In fifteen minutes its broadsides killed three men and wounded eighteen others before Chesapeake struck its flag and surrendered. Realizing this violation of another nation's sovereignty could spark a war, the British naval officers decided they could only remove certain deserters. Just four men were taken into custody. Three were subsequently confirmed as Americans, but kept imprisoned until immediately prior to war broke out in 1812. One died while in prison. The fourth man, Jenkin Ratford, was confirmed as having deserted from the naval ship Halifax on March 10, 1807. Ratford was hanged for desertion.

That the officers aboard Leopard had knowingly enlisted deserters from the Royal Navy mattered not to American public opinion. The British had fired on and boarded a U.S. naval ship. It was a grave action that could have tipped the two countries into the war that impressment and other issues threatened. But neither President Thomas Jefferson nor his Secretary of State, James Madison, would go down that road at that time. The Leopard Affair consequently was left to fester—an unresolved grievance many Americans felt keenly. In early winter of 1811, Clay returned it to the limelight by reminding Congress repeatedly that here was clear evidence that Britain did not accept America's sovereignty.

TROUBLE ON THE FRONTIER

Clay was not a man of the sea. He actually cared little about impressment or the Leopard affair. He sought war so that America could gain control of the entire North American continent. Clay was a Westerner. Kentucky stood on the edge of the American frontier. Beyond lay vast expanses of land ripe for settlement. The only thing standing between the Americans seeking new land to cultivate and otherwise exploit were Native Americans.

Since independence, Americans had been pushing relentlessly westward, driving one native tribe after another from their traditional territory. One vicious war followed another. Warriors and soldiers fought brutally. Both took scalps, butchered women and children and burned settlements. This was war without mercy, each side bent on purging the land of the other.

Clay and most Americans believed the British provided their enemy with military advice and weapons. The trade of guns, powder, and shot for fur was represented as deliberately enabling Indians to make war on American settlers. Furthermore, by 1810 the situation on the frontier had become increasingly deadly.

Having faced many serious defeats and failed to prevent ever deeper incursions by settlers into their territories, the Indians had begun setting aside inter-tribal animosities. Guided by two Shawnee brothers, each possessed of markedly contrasting but mutually charismatic personalities, an Indian confederacy had been born. Tecumseh provided the confederacy's political and military leadership. His younger brother, Tenskwatawa, provided spiritual guidance. Nicknamed the Prophet, Tenskwatawa believed he spoke directly for the Great Spirit. To gain entry to heaven, he said, the people must reject the ways of the whites.

The two brothers founded a village called Tippecanoe on the banks of the Wabash River in Indiana Territory. Their followers lived in accordance to the Prophet's teachings. Nearby whites named it Prophetstown and believed it was a place where warriors were incited and trained to make war upon them.

Tecumseh was bracing for war, but not willingly. He saw no alternative. On September 20, 1809, Indiana Governor William Henry Harrison had assembled a collection of chiefs with scant claim to legitimacy at Fort Wayne. In exchange for bribes and various trade goods, these chiefs turned 3 million acres of Indiana Territory over to the United States. The American government confirmed the Treaty of Fort Wayne as legal and binding upon the tribes its land claimed. Tecumseh warned that any whites attempting to settle in this land—where his people had taken refuge after being driven out of Ohio—would do so at risk of their lives.

As word of the treaty spread, hundreds of warriors from a mosaic of tribes gathered at Tippecanoe. Tecumseh turned to the British in Upper Canada for vitally needed supplies to feed them. Harrison was enraged when he learned that the British were providing humanitarian aid to Tecumseh's confederacy. He was equally angry that the tribes were rallying against his treaty. They were supposed to have accepted their fate. Fearing for their lives, nearby American settlers declared Prophetstown "a British scheme, and…the agents of that power are constantly exciting the Indians to hostilities against the United States." One resolution sent to Washington from Illinois called Prophetstown "the seditious village…the great nursery of hostile Indians and traitorous British Indian traders."

Harrison plotted Tippecanoe's destruction. Warriors were returning to the village from British trading posts laden with rifles, fuses, powder and lead, he claimed, and "the language and measures of the Indians indicate nothing but war." In reality, Tecumseh was trying to keep his people in check. He knew the time for war was not ripe. That time would come when the Americans inevitably declared war on Britain and he could look to Upper Canada for allies. Tecumseh could read the tide of American opinion. He heard the words of powerful men like Clay and Harrison. Men who would not stop until the United States made war on Britain and presented them with the excuse to make all North America theirs.

BATTLE OF TIPPECANOE

Governor Harrison had no intention of leaving Tippecanoe alone until Congress decided whether or not to make war on Britain. "The people of this Territory and Kentucky are extremely pressing of their service for an expedition into the Indian Country," he declared. "Any number of men might be obtained for this purpose or for a march into Canada." Even as Congress convened in Washington in November, 1811, Harrison and a thousand regular troops and militia closed on Tippecanoe. Tecumseh and many warriors were away. Working to expand the confederacy, Tecumseh had gone south to parlay with the Creek nation. On November 6, Harrison sent a message proposing negotiations. But an American deserter warned the Prophet and warrior leaders that this was a ruse and the plan was to attack at sunrise. Defending Tippecanoe with only 500 warriors was impossible, so the Prophet ordered a night assault on Harrison's camp.

Although the warriors achieved initial surprise and inflicted heavy casualties, they were ultimately routed after a two and a half hour battle. Almost a fifth of Harrison's men were killed or wounded in exchange for between 20 and 50 warriors killed. Stunned by his losses, Harrison went on the defensive rather than attack the village. On November 8, when an American patrol approached Tippecanoe, it was found abandoned.

Harrison ordered the village plundered and burned. The granary, critical to feeding the people through winter, was also destroyed. When the Americans rode away, nothing of Tippecanoe remained but ashes. In the early spring of 1812, Tecumseh stood "upon the ashes of my home" and "summoned the spirits of the braves who had fallen in their vain attempts to protect their homes from the grasping invader, and as I snuffed up the smell of their blood from the ground I swore once more eternal hatred—the hatred of an avenger."

REMEMBER TIPPECANOE!

Harrison was also calling for vengeance. Despite the fact it was he who attacked Tippecanoe, Harrison and congressmen like Clay manipulated the facts to use the losses suffered by the Americans to accuse the Indians and British of treachery. Sixty-eight Americans died in the night battle and 120 were wounded. This "blood of our murdered countrymen must be avenged," Major General Andrew Jackson wrote from his militia headquarters in Tennessee. "I do hope that Government will see that it is necessary to act efficiently and that this hostile band which must be excited to war by the secret agents of Great Britain must be destroyed." The Kentucky legislature passed a resolution blaming Great Britain for "inciting the savages…to murder the inhabitants of our defenseless frontiers—furnishing them with arms and ammunition…to attack our frontiers; to the loss of a number of brave men."

In Washington, Felix Grundy of Tennessee told his fellow congressmen that America must "drive the British from our Continent." Grundy was one of a carefully orchestrated concert of congressmen singing the tune composed by Speaker Henry Clay. Known as the War Hawks, most hailed from western states and territories. Their sole purpose during the Twelfth Congress was to force a motion of war. Driving the British from North America, Grundy said, would "ensure they no longer have an opportunity of intriguing with our Indian neighbors, and setting on the ruthless savage to tomahawk our women and children. That nation will lose her Canadian trade, and, by having no resting place in this country, her means of annoying us will be diminished."

Annoyances there were in plenty and Clay regularly stepped from the Speaker's chair to remind congress of them. Openly inciting and aiding the Indians to attack Americans on the frontier, impressment on the high seas, and the lingering aftertaste of the Leopard Affair were his favourite cards to play. But there was also the more complex orders-in-council, which was a direct affront to America's freedom of international commerce.

In a case of tit for tat, Britain and France had, over the past six years, each issued edicts intended to cripple the other's economy and ability to wage war. The edicts made it illegal for other nations to conduct business with their enemy. Any American ships entering French ports were subject to seizure by the Royal Navy, while those that ventured into British ports risked being taken by French naval vessels. As all of Europe was controlled by Napoleon's France at this time, America was effectively barred from doing business with any nations on the continent.

Hoping to force the British and French to rescind their legislation, the United States retaliated with the American Embargo Act. In its final form, the embargo cut off all American trade to Europe and the European colonies. While the embargo had a devastating impact on imports of goods to Britain, it was equally ruinous to the American economy. Overnight all cotton exports ceased. Of 46 million pounds of cotton exported annually, 80 percent went to Britain. With no provisions made to find alternative markets, textile mills across the country closed and cotton crops went unharvested for lack of any buyer. Prior to the embargo, more than half of British exports of wool and cotton products flowed to America and a quarter of its trade was with the United States. The loss of these markets threatened Britain with economic depression.

Yet the British refused to rescind the orders-in-council because it was one of few diplomatic and economic weapons it could direct against France during a time when the war with Napoleon was going badly. One after another of Britain's European allies was being forced to make peace with Napoleon after suffering defeat on the battlefield. By 1811, Britain was largely isolated and alone. And the British House of Commons was increasingly aware that it would soon have to fight another war on a battlefield across the Atlantic.

CLAY'S WAR

In Congress the debates raged on through the winter and spring of 1812. On one side were the War Hawks and most Republicans. In opposition, were the Federalists. Most Federalists were from New

England or the southern coastal slave states. Both regions depended on international trade. The orders-in-council and impressment were issues that impacted their constituents more heavily and immediately than they did the western states where the Republicans dominated. The Federalists advocated negotiation and conciliation with Britain and strongly opposed war. When they raised objection to the War Hawks, the Federalists were shouted down. No appeal to reason could counter their emotional rhetoric.

"This war, if carried successfully," Grundy stated, "will have its advantages. We shall drive the British from our continent…I therefore feel anxious not only to add the Floridas to the South, but the Canadas to the North of this empire." Britain's "outrages" against America, Clay argued, were not aimed at weakening France but to destroy the United States "as a rival…She sickens at your prosperity, and beholds in your growth—your sails spread on every ocean, and your numerous seamen, the foundations of a power which, at no very distant day, is to make her tremble for naval superiority."

Bills were passed that pushed America towards war. December 31, 1811, the president was authorized to recruit 25,000 men to the regular army. The army's purpose, Clay said, was "distinctly to be war, and war with Great Britain."   Nothing could stem the tide. Various compromises were proposed and tossed aside. Finally in May, Clay went to President Madison. A "majority of Congressmen would support war if the President recommended it," he said. On June 1, Madison did precisely that. Three days later, by a margin of 79 to 49, the House voted for war. On June 17, the Senate approved a motion for an immediate and unrestricted war on Britain by 19 to 13 votes. Madison signed the bill into law the following day. "We shall have war," Clay wrote ecstatically. "Every patriot bosom must throb with anxious solicitude for the result. Every patriot arm will assist in making that result conducive to the glory of our beloved country."

MAKING WAR, SEEKING PEACE

"At the moment of the declaration of war," Secretary of State James Monroe wrote, "the President, regretting the necessity which produced it, looked to its termination." He hoped the declaration alone would convince the British to mend their ways and seek a peace. But Madison was unaware that three weeks before he signed the war bill the British government had been thrown into disarray. On May 11, a deranged man named John Bellingham had gunned down Prime Minister Spencer Perceval. With his death, Lord Liverpool was named prime minister. Liverpool retained Viscount Castlereagh as secretary of foreign affairs. The most powerful man in the British cabinet, Castlereagh was a hard-line opponent of accommodation with the Americans over issues such as impressment. He was, however, astute enough to realize that the orders-in-council were ruining the British economy. Therefore, on the very day, Madison signed the declaration of war, Castlereagh pushed through legislation cancelling them. But America's other grievances would not be subject to negotiation. This left the United States no alternative but to actually try making war. Although authorized to raise an army of 25,000 men, that strength existed only on paper. Urged to pass a bill to greatly increase the navy's size, Congress had whittled down the number of new frigates from a requested ten, to six, then to five, four, three, and finally none at all. Only a third of existing frigates deemed unseaworthy were authorized for repair. A bill that would have armed and placed the state militias under federal control for deployment wherever the government deemed necessary was defeated.

Complaining to his old friend, and former president, Thomas Jefferson, Madison said although Congress was hell bent on enabling America to invade Canada, it had "provided, after two months delay, for a regular force requiring twelve [months] to raise it, and after three months for a volunteer force, on terms not likely to raise it at all for that object."

President Madison   *Thomas Jefferson*

On June 6, War Secretary Dr. William Eustis reported that only 5,000 men had volunteered to join the army under the new bill. That brought its total to about 11,750 officers and men. The troops were poorly trained he said, and the officers were either young and inexperienced or aged veterans of the Revolutionary War. Some states had pledged their militias, but all of New England had refused. This meant an attack against either New Brunswick or Nova Scotia was impractical, leaving Halifax—the largest British harbour in the western hemisphere—safe from either sea or land threat. Even among those states offering militia, most refused to allow them to serve beyond American borders.

The navy was in such dire condition that Secretary of the Navy Paul Hamilton proposed keeping it hidden away in safe harbours to preserve the few vessels capable of fighting. Madison would have none of it. The navy must fight and he ordered Commodore John Rodgers and Captain Stephen Decatur to put to sea in order to protect American merchantmen. Rodgers sailed from New York within ten minutes of receiving the order. He had five ships: frigates President, United States, and Congress, the sloop Hornet and the brig Argus. Rodgers was not bent on protecting American shipping. His aim was to intercept a reported British convoy of 100 merchant ships that had sailed from Jamaica for Britain. Having departed so quickly, Rodgers was long gone when revised orders directed his fleet northward with just two of the ships while Decatur patrolled the American coast in a southerly direction from New York. Learning Rodgers had already sailed, Madison and the administration were powerless to recall the impetuous and daring sailor from his self-appointed mission.

A MATTER OF MARCHING

Madison was almost as helpless when it came to directing land operations. Most Americans had agreed with Thomas Jefferson that the "acquisition of Canada this year as far as the neighbourhood of Quebec will be a mere matter of marching." But where should the army march? Major General Harry Dearborn commanded. A sixty-one-year-old veteran of the Revolution, Dearborn proposed a three-pronged invasion. A main column would advance via Lake Champlain on Montreal, a second would advance along the Niagara River and a third would sweep out of Fort Detroit into the heart of Upper Canada.

Dearborn set no timetable for these operations, so each was left to develop according to its own schedule. Nor did Dearborn have any intelligence on British strength in the Canadas. Such American intelligence estimates as there were reported regular army strength as small while the number of Royal Navy vessels on hand was such that Britain dominated the seas.

The British were actually weak on all fronts. Lieutenant General and Governor in Chief Sir George Prevost had about 5,600 regular troops available with 1,200 of these stationed in Upper Canada. Technically, in Lower Canada he could muster 60,000 militiamen, but Prevost held them in little regard. Upper Canada could provide about 10,000 militiamen, but Prevost considered only 4,000 of these worth arming. The others, he felt, were as likely to desert as fight. Prevost could rely on some support from the Indians, but it was unknown what numbers would come forward or what their fighting skill might be. Although the British navy in the western hemisphere boasted about 700 ships, only 79 were in North American waters.

Prevost expected the American main effort to fall against Upper Canada and felt his forces there were unlikely to win unless Britain sent reinforcements. He was unwilling to shift troops from Lower Canada because this would weaken his ability to defend the vital fur-trade capital of Montreal and the strategically important city of Quebec. Gloomily, he predicted that a determined American attack on Canada would succeed. The only hope of holding on to any part of the Canadas, save Quebec City, would be if the invasion was "undertaken presumptuously and without sufficient means." There was, of course, the slight chance the Americans might not invade if they were not provoked by either his forces or the Indians.

Prevost worried, however, that his Upper Canadian army commander would refuse to remain quietly on the defensive. Major General Isaac Brock had a reputation for recklessness. "Nothing should be impossible to a soldier; the word impossible should not be found in a soldier's dictionary," Brock had once said. It was a motto Brock lived by.

Major General Isaac Brock

124

He also thirsted to make a name for himself - something that could hardly be done by following Prevost's orders that nothing the Americans did would "justify offensive operations being undertaken, unless they were solely calculated to strengthen a defensive attitude."

Brock had wanted to immediately attack American's border forts. Instead, Prevost's instructions left no option but to put his troops to work strengthening the British forts that guarded the border. Brock would have to wait for the Americans to make the first move.

HULL INVADES CANADA

The force charged with attacking Upper Canada was commanded by Michigan Territory Governor William Hull. Madison had encouraged Hull to advance his troops to Fort Detroit prior to the war declaration. With little enthusiasm for his command, Hull had dithered in Urbana, Ohio. Only on June 15 did he set out with a powerful 2,000-man army to march the 185 miles north to Fort Detroit. Due to the great distances and dependence on horse couriers to pass information, Hull left Urbana unaware that the government had declared war. Not wanting to precipitate matters, Hull felt no need to hasten to the border fort. On June 26, as the army faced crossing the 50-mile-wide Black Swamp, a note from Eustis was received that urged Hull to greater haste. But the war secretary neglected to mention the war declaration.

Finally gaining the River Raisin at Frenchtown on July 2, Hull received another note from Eustis advising that America was at war and counting on him to invade Canada from Fort Detroit. As the American schooner Cayuga was in harbour at Frenchtown, Hull loaded much of the army's supplies aboard it to carry to the fort. Among the items were Hull's private papers. Cayuga was soon taken by British sailors and his papers were passed to Lieutenant Colonel Thomas St. George at Fort Malden, which lay across the border from Fort Detroit. The papers revealed Hull's entire invasion plan and detailed his army's strength and composition.

Losing any element of surprise hardly mattered because Hull had no real strategic options. On July 12 he sent troops across the Detroit River into Upper Canada and occupied the pleasant French Canadian village of Sandwich. Colonel Lewis Cass unfurled the Stars and Stripes from about his waist as he splashed ashore. As Fort Detroit's cannon loomed over the village from across the river, Brock had wisely decided against opposing the landing.

Despite the easy crossing, Hull worried. Earlier, he had attempted to win the region's Indians over or at least gain their neutrality. Tecumseh had refused to attend the meeting, but sent a message calling on them instead to rally around Britain to defeat the Americans. He closed the message by saying, "I have taken sides with the King, my father, and I will suffer my bones to bleach upon this shore before I will recross the stream to join in any council of neutrality." None of the chiefs in attendance came over to Hull's side.

Chief Tecumseh

Fearing the Indians would attack either Fort Detroit or his 200-mile-long supply line back to Urbana, Hull was reluctant to advance beyond Sandwich. He resorted to distributing fiery messages that invited Canadians to seize the moment to win their freedom from Britain by siding with America while at the same time threatening to slaughter them if they rejected this call. "No white man found fighting by the Side of an Indian will be taken prisoner. Instant destruction will be his Lot," Hull warned.

As the Indians and British were agreed on fighting at each other's side, this threat sufficiently worried enough Upper Canadians that a third of the militia quietly melted away into the night. The other two-thirds, however, were incensed by Hull's threat to grant them no quarter and expressed more determination to fight. "This is a pioneer society," one observed, "not a frontier society. No Daniel Boones stalk the Canadian forests, ready to knock off an Injun with a Kentucky rifle or do battle over an imagined slight."

Upper Canada was a peaceable place. Rather than winning the land by conquest of the Indians, Upper Canadians lived alongside them. While not an entirely harmonious relationship, there was not the hatred between whites and Indians that held sway in the United States. Each left the other mostly free to live according to their traditions.

While still refusing to budge from Sandwich, Hull unleashed his cavalry to raid nearby farms for food, equipment, and fodder for the army's animals. Every farm within 60 miles was pillaged while the farm families looked on helplessly. Brock's attempts to intercept the raiders were generally fruitless, although there were some small skirmishes. During one, Captain William McCullough became the first American to collect an Indian scalp in the campaign. He proudly wrote his wife describing how he tore the scalp from the dead warrior's head with his teeth.

The raiders stripped the farms bare, burned any crops, cut down many fruit trees, tore apart fences, and wrecked houses and outbuildings.

Having ensured the locals were now united in opposing the Americans, Hull ordered his army to erect fortifications around Sandwich while he slipped back to Fort Detroit to write reports to Washington. He complained to Eustis that his cannon were useless and he needed at least 1,500 more men to continue the invasion. Learning on July 30 that the British had seized the American Fort Mackinac at the far northern end of Lake Huron, Hull's anxiety worsened. This fort was 300 miles by boat from Fort Detroit and the British forces responsible for its capture could not possibly threaten him. But the fort's fall had coincided with the sudden move of the Wyandot tribe across the Detroit River and into British lines. Hull imagined hundreds of Indians were massing to massacre his army.

His worst fears seemed realized when Tecumseh and a raiding party ambushed a supply column coming to Fort Detroit from Urbana on August 5. Three days later, Hull ordered Sandwich abandoned and withdrew his army behind the walls of Fort Detroit.

Realizing that Hull and his army were thoroughly demoralized, Brock decided the time to defeat the Americans was at hand. Brock arrived at Fort Malden with 50 regulars, 250 Canadian militia, and a 6-pound cannon. Here Tecumseh and Brock met for the first time.

When Tecumseh's warriors fired their muskets to salute Brock's arrival, the British general quietly told the warrior leader that this was "really an unnecessary waste of ammunition when Detroit had to be captured." Tecumseh turned to his warriors and said, "This is a man." Brock concluded of Tecumseh that "a more sagacious or a more gallant Warrior does not I believe exist." These two kindred fighters set siege to Fort Detroit on August 16 with 300 regulars, 400 militia, 30 artillerymen manning 5 cannon, and 600 warriors. Brock sent a message warning that if Hull did not surrender, the British could not control the warriors and a massacre was inevitable.

The meeting of Tecumseh and Isaac Brock

As Brock's troops advanced the following morning, Hull hoisted a flag of truce and quickly surrendered. Some 1,600 Ohio militia were paroled home while Hull and 582 regular army soldiers were marched to prisoner-of-war camps near Quebec City. This bloodless victory left the British in undisputed control of the Upper Canadian frontier.

FALTERING NEGOTIATIONS

Despite the first American attempt on the Canadas ending in resounding defeat, President Madison and Secretary of State Monroe decided that peace was only possible if the British ceased impressment. "Having gone to war, it seemed to be our duty, not to withdraw from it, till the rights of our country were placed on a more secure basis," Monroe explained.
At the same time, Prevost was still trying to keep the war from escalating. Upon learning that the orders-in-council had been cancelled, he thought the Americans would willingly agree to negotiations. Prevost sent an emissary to meet with Dearborn at his headquarters near Albany, New York. Prevost offered a ceasefire that Dearborn readily accepted.

Since being appointed to command the army, Dearborn had approached the task with a complete lack of enthusiasm. A "ponderous, flabby figure, weighing two hundred and fifty pounds," Dearborn was nicknamed Granny by his troops. By the time the ceasefire was agreed on August 9, he had succeeded in only recruiting a mere 1,200 men from the New England states and was woefully short of the strength needed to invade Lower Canada.

It took six days for Dearborn's report of the ceasefire to reach Washington. Madison was infuriated and War Secretary Eustis immediately replied that Dearborn was to advise Prevost that the ceasefire was over. Eustis told Dearborn to "proceed with the utmost vigor in your operations." He demanded that Dearborn immediately capture the towns of Niagara and Kingston. This would cut Upper Canada off from Lower Canada.

Chastened, Dearborn reported that he would "push towards Montreal at the same time that our troops on the western frontier of this state strike at Upper Canada." These two operations would begin in

October. Madison, meanwhile, had learned of Hull's surrender. He had expected Hull to easily take Upper Canada and transform Lake Erie into an American pond. A British defeat would have left the Indians "neutral or submissive to our will," he said, and prompted thousands of Americans to enlist. Instead, Hull had "sunk before obstacles at which not an officer near him would have paused, and threw away an entire army." The surrender would surely turn "the people of Canada…against us" and encourage more native tribes to join the British. "A general damp spread over our Affairs," Madison wrote.

QUEENSTON HEIGHTS

The American forces facing Niagara Peninsula were gathered at Lewiston, New York—three hundred miles west of Dearborn's headquarters near Albany. Deciding that the rigors of such a journey would be too much for him, Dearborn sent Virginian General Alexander Smyth with vague instruction that he was to share command with New York General Stephen Van Rensselaer. Smyth marched to Lewiston with 1,650 regulars to reinforce the 3,000 troops already there.

An unwilling political appointee, Van Rensselaer was a Federalist opposed to the war. Most of his troops were New York Republicans, who could scarce believe he was in charge. Van Rensselaer had surrounded himself with Federalist-inclined officers and kept himself distant from the rank and file. Lacking military experience, he leaned heavily on his cousin and aide-de-camp Lieutenant Colonel Solomon Van Rensselaer for guidance. None of the senior officers supported the war or were inclined to get on with attacking Niagara. Instead, upon learning of Hull's surrender, Van Rensselaer became convinced that he was being set up by the Republican administration in Washington. Were he to attack and fail, Van Rensselaer believed he would be made a scapegoat for the administration's botched prosecution of the war.

When Smyth reached Buffalo, south of Lewiston, on September 29, Van Rensselaer's suspicion that he was the victim of a Republican conspiracy deepened. Smyth, for his part, refused to advance his men from Buffalo to Lewiston. Instead, the two officers bickered by letter over where the army should cross the Niagara River and who would command. The Van Rensselaers were agreed that the best crossing point was at Queenston Heights where British defences were weak due to the natural barrier of rapids. It was the anticipation of attacking here that had led Van Rensselaer to situate his troops in Lewiston, directly opposite Queenston. Smyth argued that the better crossing point was at Buffalo, although the British had stronger defences on the opposite shore.

Van Rensselaer finally decided to break the stalemate by attacking independent of Smyth. On October 10, he ordered his men to prepare to cross the turbulent waters in boats after nightfall. The long delay had enabled Major General Brock to travel from Detroit to Niagara to oversee its defence. He had 400 regulars, 800 militiamen, and 200 Indian warriors. The militiamen had only returned to duty after bringing in their harvests and were exhausted. Morale amongst the regulars of the 49th Foot was so low after months of inactivity that the men were in a mutinous state. Brock realized his forces were desperately thin on the ground—a problem exacerbated by his uncertainty over where the Americans were likely to strike. Although the Americans were split between Buffalo and Lewiston, Brock thought neither location a likely launching point. If he were in charge, Brock would force a crossing upstream where the river was narrower. So he split the majority of his forces between Chippewa and Fort Erie in anticipation of the Americans doing the sensible thing.

The battle would be decided right on the river bank, Brock either winning a decisive victory or going down in bloody defeat. "I say decisive," he wrote his brother, "because if I should be beaten, the province is inevitably gone, and should I be victorious, I do not imagine the gentry from the other side will be anxious to return to the charge."

During the night of October 10–11, an assault force attempted to cross in front of Queenston only to discover that the boat carrying the oars for the entire fleet had drifted downstream and run aground. Van Rensselaer ordered the operation set back forty-eight hours.

At three in the morning on August 13, the 600 troops in the assault wave boarded thirteen boats and began rowing across the river under cover of a heavy artillery bombardment. Three boats carrying about 200 men were swept downstream and out of the fight, but the remaining ten gained the opposing shore. A mere 46 regulars and handful of Canadian militia met them with musket fire. No army in the world could match the British soldier's rate of musketry - two shots a minute.

Solomon Van Rensselaer fell critically wounded. The musket fire was withering while from high up on the cliff of Queenston Heights cannon lashed the Americans with canister shot that sprayed them with lethal bits of iron. With the attack faltering, Captain John E. Wool led 60 men along the shoreline in search of a rumoured trail that led to the summit.

Brock and his aide, Lieutenant Colonel John Macdonell, meanwhile, had been awakened by the cannon fire. They galloped to Queenston, picking up troops and militia along the way. Arriving at dawn, Brock saw a second wave of Americans in boats on the water. He reached the cannon battery on the summit just as Wool's Americans broke from the trees. Brock ordered the guns spiked and the gunners to retreat to Queenston village.

As the second wave of Americans tumbled from their boats, the battle hung in the balance. Jumping from his horse, Brock formed 100 regulars and an equal number of militiamen into line and ordered an advance up the steep slope of the heights. A musket ball tore open Brock's wrist, but he continued to walk toward the Americans. When the British and Canadians were 165 feet from the American line, Brock ordered them to fix bayonets and charge. As he rushed forward, sword held high, an American scout rose from nearby bushes and fired a ball from his long musket that struck Brock in the chest just above the heart.

The attack broke with Brock's death. Gathering their fallen commander, the men began retreating. They were well along when Macdonell came towards them with a small number of militiamen in tow. Managing to rally about 70 militia and regulars, Macdonell ordered a new charge. "Revenge the General," the men yelled as they lunged towards the several hundred Americans on the summit of Queenston Heights. Moments later Macdonell was mortally wounded and the attack collapsed. The survivors withdrew northward from Queenston to Vrooman's Point.

Here they were joined by Major General Roger Sheaffe, who had under his command 300 regulars, 250 militiamen, and an artillery battery. Within several hours Sheaffe's force had grown to more than 400 regulars, an equal number of militia, and 300 Mohawk warriors. Although still outnumbered by the Americans on the heights, who had used the time to erect fortifications, Sheaffe ordered another attack.

Sheaffe expected to fail. But he was unaware that the Americans were badly disorganized and demoralized. At Lewiston hundreds of New York militia had asserted their right to refuse to serve beyond the nation's borders. They sat on the river bank to watch the battle like spectators at a sports event. Only 350 American regulars and 250 New Yorkers were on the heights.

When the Mohawks snuck up behind the Americans and attacked, they wheeled to meet the threat. This left them with backs turned to Sheaffe's main force. After the men fired a musket volley, Sheaffe ordered a bayonet charge. As the British and Canadians ran forward the Americans fled. Most were unable to regain the boats and escape. More than 300 were killed or wounded and 958 surrendered. British and Canadian losses totaled only 14 dead, 77 wounded and 21 missing. But Brock's death was sorely felt and also meant the man most capable of defending Canada was lost.

Brock's death, however, galvanized Upper Canadian opposition to the Americans. More than 5,000 militiamen attended his funeral on October 16 at Niagara. Sheaffe reported to Prevost that no longer were Upper Canadian militiamen failing to turn out for duty. Rather they were coming forward to volunteer and were "very alert at their several posts and continue generally to evince the best dispositions."

Not so across the river. The New York militia bluntly refused to consider advancing into Upper Canada. Van Rensselaer was recalled and Smyth given full command. But he could do nothing. The American campaigns against the Canadas were at a standstill.

BRITISH REVERSES AT SEA

Because news from North America could only be transmitted to Britain by slow sailing ships, reports of Brock's victory at Fort Detroit arrived at the same time as he was killed at Queenston. Secretary of War and Colonial Office Sir Henry Bathurst and his Colonial Office Undersecretary John Goulburn were relieved to finally receive some good news regarding the war with America. Correspondence from Prevost had been consistently grim and pessimistic. Prevost complained of endless shortages in equipment, supplies and men. He feared the Indian warriors would meet American aggression with wanton and unnecessary bloodshed that would make negotiating a peace settlement impossible.

As Bathurst was preoccupied with the war against France, it fell to Goulburn to handle Britain's response to the war with America. In fact, the twenty-eight year old was effectively in charge of running the British Empire. Bright and articulate, Goulburn believed the reasons offered by President Madison for declaring war camouflaged America's true intentions. These were to conquer the

Canadas and gain control of all North America. This would be followed by the eventual genocide of all the Indian peoples. Goulburn further thought that any unnecessary bloodshed would result more often from American action rather than the Indians. He advised Prevost that the Indian warriors could be kept in check if they were commanded by British or Canadian officers experienced in working with them.

Goulburn also sent practical help in the form of two heavily laden supply ships to Canada and sufficient clothing and equipment to supply another 800 British regulars. Prevost was also permitted to promise that every colonist who chose to join the army would be granted 100 acres of land. Finally, he wanted Prevost to think less about negotiating peace than making war. Although so far victorious on land, the war was proving a disaster at sea.

The British took great pride in their navy, believing it could never be beaten. Yet through the late summer and fall the Americans had inflicted a series of stinging defeats that threatened to shatter this myth of invincibility. On August 19, the frigate Guerrière had been sunk by the Constitution about 400 miles south of Newfoundland. Constitution was commanded by Captain Isaac Hull, whose uncle had surrendered Fort Detroit just four days earlier. Its crew numbered 460 serving 55 guns compared to Guerrière's 49 guns and 280-man crew. But Captain James R. Dacre expected British superiority in seamanship and fighting ability would carry the day. Hull had trained his crew to a standard of accuracy the British could not match. In the ensuing close-range duel Guerrière lost most of its sails and rigging.
After 15 men were killed and 63 wounded, Dacre ordered the ship's colours struck. Constitution had only 7 sailors killed and 7 wounded. Guerrière was so badly damaged Hull had to take the British crew aboard and then burn the listing hulk.

This defeat was just the beginning. When Commodore John Rodgers returned to America after a 70-day voyage that ultimately took him to within sight of the English coast, he sailed into port with seven British merchant ships in tow. Then, on October 8, the British brig Frolic was captured by the American sloop Wasp near the West Indies. Although the arrival of the far larger ship of the line Poitiers later that day reversed the situation with Wasp surrendering and Frolic being freed, once again British invincibility was thrown into question.

Public morale in Britain was noticeably shaken by the realization that the nation's merchant fleet was no longer safe to ply the seas without fear of interception by American ships. It was also clear that the Royal Navy could be bested. In America, however, public opinion was increasingly opposed to the war. No victories at sea could make up for the defeats on land. President Madison was blamed for starting the war and for its poor prosecution.

A DISMAL WINTER

Not only did Madison have to fight a war in the fall and winter of 1812, but he was also running for re-election as president. His opponent was a fellow Republican, but one whose support came from the New England and other northern states where the war was unpopular. Madison's support was concentrated in the southern and western frontier states. Madison had hoped that the campaign against the Canadas could be rekindled in the last months of the year. But military developments had been little short of a joke.

Facing Niagara Peninsula, General Alexander Smyth had been urged to take Fort Erie. But after making a half-hearted effort and being repulsed, Smyth had stood the army down for the winter. He then got permission from Dearborn to visit his family in Virginia. Smyth headed south with no intention of ever returning.

Dearborn, meanwhile, finally gathered 3,000 regulars and an equal number of militia at Plattsburgh, New York and marched on Montreal in mid-November. The army was detected by French-Canadian scouts the moment it entered Lower Canada. Major Charles-Michel d'Irumberry de Salaberry of the French Canadian Provincial Corps of Light Infantry moved to meet it with just two small companies of Voltigeurs and 300 Indian warriors. After a short skirmish on November 20, where confused American troops fired on each other, Dearborn withdrew to Plattsburgh.

AMERICAN SUPREMACY ON THE LAKES

One thing Madison had always understood was the importance of controlling the Great Lakes. But America had entered the war ill prepared to gain their mastery. If the British lost the ability to move men and supplies freely by water, they would be less able to defend their communities and forts scattered along the shorelines. Lying as it did at the nexus of Lower and Upper Canada, Lake Ontario was the most strategically vital lake. On September 3, Madison had ordered Commodore Isaac

Chauncey to gain control of it. Chauncey raised his flag at Sackets Harbour on the southeastern shore and studied the ships under his command. Only one—the brig Oneida—was a war ship. The others were converted lake schooners.

Undaunted, Chauncey sallied with Oneida and six schooners against the British corvette Royal George. Outnumbered, the ship fled into Kingston Harbour. Unable to press the attack because of cannon fire from the town's fort, Chauncey withdrew. Chauncey rightly claimed that he controlled Lake Ontario and pointed to the refusal of the British ships in Kingston to come out and fight.

On both sides, meanwhile, a fierce race began as boat builders sought to construct bigger, more powerful ships to go into service with the spring. The Americans launched Madison, a 24-gun corvette that was the largest ship on the lake, in November. They also laid the keel of General Pike, another even larger 26-gun corvette. British boat-building efforts were hampered by lack of material and poor management. But work at York on a large frigate named Sir Isaac Brock was underway and repairs were also started on an old schooner, Duke of Gloucester.

Both the British and Americans were also busy on fleets for Lake Erie. The Americans soon had a larger fleet there than the British. But these ships were based in the harbour of Presque Isle in Pennsylvania. This harbour was sheltered by a long sandbar covered at high tide by six and a half feet of water. The American brigs required ten feet of draft so could only depart via a narrow opening that the British quickly blockaded. So long as they kept ships outside the harbour, the Americans were trapped.

FLAMES ON THE FRONTIER

Brock's victory at Fort Detroit had encouraged many tribes that had earlier been bullied into treaties by Indiana Governor William Henry Harrison to rise up against the Americans. When the Potawatomi laid siege to Fort Wayne, Tecumseh marched from Canada with a large force to turn the uprising into a general war on the frontier. He expected the British to follow, but only about 500 men under Major Adam Muir were sent. Even these were committed reluctantly because Prevost believed any advance across the American border might derail a negotiated peace.

Tecumseh's forces were formidable but badly scattered. Harrison, meanwhile, commanded a larger, better equipped army of Kentucky militia and regular troops. With 2,000 men, Harrison broke the siege of Fort Wayne and the Indian warriors melted into the forests. As winter set in, Indians and Americans became locked in a vicious frontier battle neither side could win.

Hoping to break the deadlock, Harrison tried to regain Fort Detroit and capture Fort Malden across the river. With 6,300 men, he marched through bitter winter conditions. To clear the way to Detroit, Harrison sent Brigadier General James Winchester ahead with 1,000 men. On January 18, 1813, Winchester's men drove 50 Canadian militiamen and 100 Indians away from Frenchtown on the Raisin River. With Detroit just 26 miles distant and believing he owned the field, Winchester failed to erect any defensive fortifications or send out patrols.

Just before dawn on January 22, the Americans awoke to an attack by 600 redcoats and militia commanded by Lieutenant Colonel William Procter and 700 Indian warriors under Tecumseh. This force had crossed Lake Erie on the ice from Fort Malden during a night march.

In the ensuing battle, 397 Americans were killed and 536, including Winchester, taken prisoner. Lacking sufficient soldiers to guard all the prisoners, Procter left 30 of the most seriously wounded under Indian guard at Frenchtown while he withdrew his force and the other prisoners to Brownstown. Soon a group of Indians drunk on captured liquor pushed the guard aside and scalped the helpless prisoners. When word of these murders reached Washington, the political slogan and rallying cry, "Remember the Raisin River," was born.

STALEMATE IN WASHINGTON

On December 3, Madison had been re-elected president with a sweeping majority, but he faced a Congress and Senate opposed to any legislation that would enable him to make war more effectively. A bill to raise the army from its current 19,000 to 30,000 was stonewalled by demands for more information. Nor would Congress approve forcing state militias to serve wherever they were sent. When Secretary of the Treasury Albert Gallatin tabled a series of proposals aimed at financing the war, Congress defeated them all. Yet, led by Speaker Henry Clay, Congress continued to declare its determination that the war proceed. Victory just had to be won without much cost to the taxpayer. The only concession the administration won was a bill authorizing increasing the army by 20,000 more men to a total strength of about 35,000. These men, however, would not be required to sign on for the customary five years. Instead, they need agree to only twelve months service. Congress was gambling on winning the war in a year.

Desperate for good news, Madison was delighted to report to Congress on February 22 that the navy had once again won a success. On December 29, Constitution had intercepted the 49-gun Java and sunk her. But Madison also knew the navy could not alone bring Britain to its knees. There were not enough ships for America to gain mastery of the seas. The conquest of Canada was to have provided a bargaining chip that could be exchanged for an honourable peace. But Madison doubted the 1813 campaign season would see his army succeed. A protracted war that the nation could not afford loomed.

Consequently, when the Russian minister to America came to Madison's home on March 6 with a note from Tsar Alexander I offering to act as peacemaker between American and Britain, the president grabbed at the proposal like a drowning man grasping a lifeline. The Russian emperor's offer was "humane and enlightened," he said. And Russia was "the only power in Europe which can command respect from both France and England."

THE TSAR'S PEACE INITIATIVE

Tsar Alexander had first considered playing the role of peacemaker between America and Britain in September, 1812. This was even as Moscow fell to Napoleon's Grand Armée and the Russian people feared his troops might soon be marching through the capital of Saint Petersburg. Alexander, however, was unafraid. He knew the French were badly overextended. Napoleon's supply lines were not secure. As the Russians had retreated, they burned crops and food supplies. The French were currently victorious but were also hungry, exhausted, short on ammunition and increasingly fewer in number. Winter was closing in and the French were ill prepared to endure its harsh conditions. Alexander expected winter to break the French and he was correct. By the time his offer to act as an intermediary reached Madison, the French were gone from Russia. It was also clear that the French were no longer dominant in Europe. In fact, they were on the retreat and Alexander expected Napoleon's full defeat in 1813. His reasons for seeking a peace between America and Britain were twofold. First, Alexander wanted to increase his reputation on the world stage. Second, the war was harming Russian commerce. Alexander had first raised the subject with America's minister to Russia, John Quincy Adams, in the fall of 1812. Adams had been intrigued and asked Washington whether he should participate if the British agreed. The British representative, Lord Cathcart, had also sought instruction from London.

By February, 1813 it was clear that Britain was winning the war with France and Adams thought it increasingly impossible that America could prevail on the battlefield. He told one Russian adviser that Americans were "all too raw and unskilled in war to make much progress in Canada." The losses the U.S. Navy had inflicted at sea had only "mortified [Britain's] national pride, and touched their point of honor in its tenderest part...and would make them think they must now fight not only for their honor, but for revenge."

In Washington, Madison also realized France was losing its war with Britain. Time was running out to either prevail on the battlefield or try to negotiate a peace before the war turned too far against America. Once peace came to Europe, Britain would be free to send massive naval and army reinforcement to Canada and any hope of victory would be lost. Also, once the European war ended, the only remaining argument upon which the declaration of war had been based would disappear. The orders-in-council were already gone. Impressment would end when the Royal Navy no longer required large numbers of sailors. Madison wanted to secure a negotiated peace before America was left fighting a war without cause.

Deciding to immediately send envoys to join Adams in St. Petersburg, Madison selected his treasurer, Albert Gallatin, and the Federalist senator from Delaware, James Bayard. Sending one of his most respected political opponents would demonstrate the sincerity of his peace quest. The two envoys sailed for Russia on May 11.

BRITAIN'S HARDENING RESOLVE.

In Britain, the war with America was no longer a sideshow to the war with France. Goulburn had raised a large number of army reinforcements to send to Canada. Many, however, would have to first be collected from all points of the Empire and Goulburn could offer no promises on the number who would arrive in time for the 1813 campaign season. It was possible that Governor General Prevost would be forced to fight with only the men in hand.

To force America to divert troops from Canada, Admiral Sir John Warren was ordered to send ships out from Halifax to raid America's coastline. By early spring, Warren had blockaded Chesapeake and Delaware bays, New York City, Charleston, Port Royal, Savannah, and the mouth of the Mississippi. No American ships were allowed in or out and were seized if possible. Neutral ships were warned off and any within these harbours were denied exit.

America's navy was too weak to challenge these blockades, but a good number of its war ships managed to escape to sea. Others had already been loose before the blockades were established. In February, the 18-gun sloop Hornet mauled and sunk the British brig Peacock in the south Atlantic. Spring 1813 found the 32-gun Essex spreading terror among a British whaling fleet operating off the Galapagos Islands.

The British, meanwhile, launched their first raid within Chesapeake Bay on April 28. Admiral Sir George Cockburn landed 180 seamen, 200 marines and a small artillery detachment that struck Frenchtown on the Elk River. After burning a large quantity of military stores and several vessels, the force escaped with only one man having been wounded. Cockburn went on to destroy an artillery battery at Havre de Grace five days later and raided Georgetown and Fredericktown on the Sassafras River on May 5. The British reported never having seen a coast so undefended and Warren increased Cockburn's forces by 2,400 men to intensify raiding operations.

On June 1, the Americans attempted to regain the initiative when Captain James Lawrence aboard Chesapeake challenged Captain Philip Broke of the Shannon to a head-to-head battle outside Boston harbour. Both ships mounted 38 guns and about the same number of crew. A fierce fight ensued during which Lawrence was wounded in the leg by a sniper's musket ball. Then the two ships collided and British sailors swarmed the American ship. Lawrence was wounded a second time when a bullet pierced his abdomen. As Broke led even more British sailors on to Chesapeake, the dying Lawrence cried, "Don't give up the ship!" But it was too late, the surviving American officer surrendered. Broke, too, lay dying along with 23 other British sailors. Another 58 were wounded. The Americans had lost 61 killed and 85 wounded. Chesapeake was taken to Halifax and Lawrence was buried there with full military honours.

This naval victory did much to quell public criticism, but it was the raids on American soil that were more strategically worthwhile. Raids through June and July spread terror along the American coastline.

RAIDS ON THE LAKES

The Americans were also proving capable of launching devastating raids but on the Great Lakes instead of at sea. On April 27, a 14-ship American squadron carrying 1,700 infantry had struck the shipbuilding facilities at York. Seriously outnumbered, Major General Roger Sheafe withdrew his 600 men rather than fight. He also burned an unfinished ship and blew up a large ammunition magazine. The ensuing explosion injured 250 Americans, 38 of whom died. Angry at their losses, the Americans looted the town, vandalized property and bullied unarmed citizens. They also burned the legislative building, Government House and most military barracks. After confiscating large amounts of military stores, the Americans set sail.

Commodore Isaac Chauncey, who had commanded the naval part of the operation, had once again proven that his ships controlled Lake Ontario. This positioned the Americans well for land operations against Niagara Peninsula and even Kingston. At Sackets Harbor, Major General Henry Dearborn had 4,000 soldiers and it had been part of this force that participated in the York raid. Another 3,000 men were assembled at Buffalo. After the raid on York, Chauncey was to transport the men at Sackets Harbor to carry out an amphibious assault on Fort George while the troops at Buffalo attacked it by land. On May 25, after Chauncey's ships subjected the fort to a heavy bombardment, the British regulars and Canadian militia there withdrew to a new position near Beaver Dams.
The raid on York and the fall of Fort George were serious defeats that left the British soldiers and Canadian settlers fearing that Niagara Peninsula might be entirely lost.

BRITAIN'S TENUOUS HOLD

In 1813 the thin line of Red defending Canada was stretched to the limit. There were little more than 9,000 troops in all the Canadas and 2,000 of these were provincials considered of dubious quality. Militia call-ups in May had not yielded the high reporting levels Prevost had hoped for. Most militia-

140

men were farmers and it was a difficult choice to don a uniform instead of sowing the seed required to produce crops necessary to feed their families. The winter just passed had seen food shortages in some regions. With this year's campaign season expected to be longer and more extensive than in 1812, there was much talk of possible famines in Upper Canada if crops went unplanted or harvested because the men were off fighting. Many American settlers, who had come to Upper Canada for cheap land and the security the British offered against Indian wars, packed their bags and drifted back into the United States.

Everywhere Prevost looked American troops gathered and he had little confidence they could be held back. In the west, newly promoted Major General Henry Harrison had built a major fort called Fort Meigs just below the Maumee Rapids to serve as a base. At Presque Isle, Captain Oliver Hazard Perry continued work on the ships that could challenge British supremacy on Lake Erie the moment an opportunity to slip past the blockade occurred.

From Amherstburg, the also newly promoted Brigadier General Henry Procter watched these developments with growing concern. Procter was caught in a dilemma. He lacked men and supplies necessary to go on the offensive, but Tecumseh was unwilling to accept a purely defensive strategy. Without Indian support, the British could never retain the Upper Canadian frontier, so Procter agreed to a limited operation intended to seize Fort Meigs.

On April 28, Procter loaded 550 regulars, 464 militia, and 63 fencibles aboard two gunboats, six other vessels, and a flotilla of bateaux and crossed the lake to the mouth of the Maumee River. They were joined there by Tecumseh and 1,500 warriors. Soon British gun batteries and the gunboats were pounding the unfinished fort in an attempt to force Harrison's surrender. Harrison was determined to hold out because reinforcements were on the way. In the early morning hours of May 5, 1,200 Kentucky troops shot the rapids in boats and overran the British gun batteries. Prevost counterattacked with the 41st Regiment's regulars supported by Tecumseh's warriors and broke the Kentucky line. The Americans suffered 836 casualties in exchange for only 101 British casualties.

Once again some American prisoners were killed and scalped by renegade Indians before Tecumseh could bring them under control. Procter continued the siege until May 9 when the militiamen left to sow their crops and he realized it would be impossible to force Harrison to surrender. The withdrawal left Harrison still threatening the frontier, but he remained on the defensive. Harrison was waiting for

Perry to finish his ships at Presque Isle. Perry was building two brigs, Lawrence and Niagara. Weighing 500 tons and mounting two masts with square sails, each was fitted with eighteen 32-pounder carronades and two long 12-pounder guns. Perry also had eight smaller schooners, some built from scratch and others, like Caledonia, that had been captured from the British. His biggest problem was a lack of sailors to crew the vessels. But if he could get past the British blockade of Presque Isle and onto the lakes with even a few ships, Perry could then support Harrison in an amphibious operation.

PREVOST ATTACKS SACKETS HARBOR

While the Americans had been seizing Fort George on Niagara Peninsula, Prevost had used the opportunity of their being at the opposite end of Lake Ontario to assault Sackets Harbor. He hoped to destroy the shipbuilding facilities and regain control of the lake. With 800 men, Prevost sailed from Kingston on May 25. Arriving just before nightfall, Prevost decided to keep his men aboard in the dark, damp holds rather than attack immediately. Come morning, dispirited and weary British troops landed and were met by 500 American militiamen. After three hours of fighting and with his troops gaining the upper hand, Prevost suddenly lost his nerve and ordered a retreat. The raid had achieved nothing, but it succeeded in panicking the Americans into pulling back into Sackets Harbor to defend the new corvette that was under construction. Suddenly the British were again masters of Lake Ontario.

LAURA SECORD TO THE RESCUE

Unable to move men by ship, Dearborn sent his army marching into Upper Canada. Claiming ill health, Dearborn directed two other generals to lead the 3,500 troops without specifying which of them was in charge. Both men were cautious by nature so the advance progressed slowly. On June 5, the Americans arrived at Stoney Creek and encamped for the night. British scouts prowled about the camp in the night and determined that the two generals had failed to tie their respective forces together. A hasty attack by Lieutenant Colonel John Harvey and 700 men at 11:30 that night threw the American camp into chaos.

Both generals were captured along with about 100 troops. Although British casualties of 214 proved higher than the American loses of 168, morning found the redcoats holding the field. The Americans retired to Fort George. Dearborn handed command to Brigadier General John Boyd. Determined to return to the offensive, Boyd decided to march on the outpost at Beaver Dam. This small outpost was commanded by Lieutenant James FitzGibbon and meant to protect a settlement of Mohawk and Caughnawaga Indians. Boyd ordered Lieutenant Colonel Charles Boerstler to take 700 men to over-run the outpost and then attack the Indian encampment.

Boerstler set out on June 23, advancing through heavy rain as far as Queenston. Here thirty-five-year-old Laura Secord learned of the American plan and trekked through the night to warn FitzGibbon. The lieutenant alerted the Indians and an ambush was set. At nine o'clock the next morning the Americans struggling up the muddy road were ambushed from behind by 300 Caughnawaga and 100 Mohawks. After three hours of fighting, the demoralized Americans were ready to surrender but feared being massacred. That was when FitzGibbon and 50 redcoats advanced and the Americans rushed to be taken under their protection. While the American militiamen were paroled, 462 officers and regular army troops were taken prisoner.

After this defeat, Dearborn refused to stir again from Fort George. He expected to be attacked by superior forces at any moment. When a message arrived from Washington relieving him of command, Dearborn was content to go. Major General James Wilkinson was appointed to replace him. But the new commander, another Revolutionary War veteran, was in Georgia and did not arrive in Washington until early August. The summer months of 1813 passed on the Canadian border with the Americans doing little. A stalemate existed. Nothing had advanced the American cause.

BRITISH DEFEATS ON THE FRONTIER

After Sheafe fled York, Prevost had relieved him and appointed Major General Francis de Rotten-burg as Upper Canada's British commander. De Rottenburg pessimistically expected the Americans to gain control of Lake Ontario. In that event, he planned to withdraw from Niagara Peninsula and fall back to Kingston. De Rottenburg advised Major General Henry Procter that he would also have to escape via Lake Huron to Lake Superior. Procter was shocked by this instruction. He immediately wrote Prevost to warn that should the British abandon Lake Erie they would lose the support of Tecumseh's confederacy.

Since the failure at Fort Meigs, relations between Procter and Tecumseh had soured. Tecumseh blamed the defeat on Procter and wanted to attack the fort again or attempt to destroy the ships at Presque Isle. When the two met to discuss strategy, however, Procter proposed instead attacking Fort Stephenson on the Sandusky River because it would be easier to capture.

Tecumseh saw no sense in this scheme. At Fort Meigs 2,000 American troops were under command of Brigadier General Green Clay. Nine miles up the Sandusky River, Harrison had another 2,000 men camped at Seneca Town. Tecumseh had about 3,000 warriors and believed he could defeat either American force so long as they were not allowed to come together.

Procter finally agreed to another attempt on Fort Meigs, but he committed just 300 men and a few guns. On July 25, the British and Tecumseh's warriors approached Fort Meigs in a vast flotilla of canoes and boats. Tecumseh had hoped to lure Clay into coming out of the fort, but the American refused to be drawn. After two fruitless days, Tecumseh agreed to march with Procter on Fort Stephenson. The fort's garrison consisted of just 160 regulars under Major George Croghan. They had a single 6-pound gun.

American scouts following the thousands of Indians marching towards Fort Stephenson alerted Harrison, who ordered Croghan to withdraw to Seneca Town. Croghan replied that there was not enough time to retreat and that he had "determined to maintain this place and by heaven we can." Rather than facing Tecumseh and his thousands, Croghan ended up under siege by just Procter's troops and 300 warriors. The rest, including Tecumseh drifted off during the march because they saw no point in the attack. After shelling the fort for several hours on August 1, Procter attacked. To gain the palisade walls required entering a deep ditch that surrounded the fort. Once his troops and warriors were inside it they were subjected to withering musket fire and blasts of grapeshot from the single cannon. Unable to scale the walls, the attack crumbled. The warriors broke off first, fleeing into the woods. Of the 250 British who had gone into the attack, 96 were killed or wounded.

Procter fell back to Amherstburg where he attempted to justify the attack as required to keep the

Indians committed to Britain. Prevost slammed him for losing so many men in a pointless operation and urged him to instead concentrate on working with Lake Erie's British naval commander, Captain Robert Barclay, to maintain control of its waters and coastline. This, he said, is what Commodore James Yeo had done successfully on Lake Ontario.

PROWLING LAKE ONTARIO

Throughout July the British on Lake Ontario had been trying unsuccessfully to draw the Americans out of Sackets Harbor, yet clearly a fight to decide ownership of the lake was inevitable. Although the British had six warships of varying classes and well-trained crews that could hold a formation together, their guns were all carronades—short-ranged cannon that fired heavy shot. The American ships were a hodgepodge. Ten civilian schooners fitted with cannon and only three corvettes that were truly warships. Crews were poorly trained and the variety of ships and their sails made it all but impossible to maintain formation. All the American ships, however, mounted long guns that were long-ranged and fired lighter shot than a carronade. The Americans hoped to sink the British at a distance before the carronades came within range to smash their ships with their heavier shot.

The Americans had one other advantage—the most powerful ship on the lake. General Pike was big. It had a crew of 300 and mounted 26 guns that fired 24-pound shot. A single broadside could devastate any British ship that came within range. On July 20, General Pike ventured out with the rest of the fleet following. About 2,000 sailors manned the ships and on board were 2,000 soldiers. Their intent was to assault the British supply depot at Burlington. Finding the town too well defended, the Americans again raided York on July 31. After returning the troops to Fort Niagara, the American fleet turned about to find the British waiting with two corvettes, two brigs, and two large schooners. After much maneuvering and without either side suffering much damage, the ships were suddenly caught in a gale at two in the morning of August 8. Two American schooners capsized and were lost.

When the storm abated, the two opponents continued to circle each other while seeking an advantage. Finally two schooners, Growler and Julia, drifted free of the American line and all six British ships closed and forced their surrender. But the surviving Americans continued to refuse battle, each side warily circling the other well into September without a decisive action.

DECISION ON LAKE ERIE

Believing the Americans still not ready to sail, the British blockading Presque Isle withdrew from August 2 to 4 in order to resupply. The Americans seized the moment. Lawrence and Niagara sailed out on August 5. Facing a shortage of sailors, the British withdrew and set frantically to finishing construction of the brig Detroit. The Americans, meanwhile, established their fleet at Put-in-Bay, about 30 miles from Amherstburg and sailed back and forth in front of the town and nearby Fort Malden to prove their supremacy over the lake. On September 9, the British decided the time to act had come and emerged with the brigs Detroit, Queen Charlotte, and Lady Prevost, and three schooners. Plagued by weak winds that made movement sluggish, the two forces were soon locked in battle. The U.S. flagship, Lawrence, was eventually so badly shot up that the fleet commander escaped by rowboat to Niagara and the surviving crew surrendered.

Aboard Detroit, the British commander had been wounded in the leg. Then a volley of canister inflicted a massive shoulder wound that knocked him unconscious just as Queen Charlotte collided with Detroit and the rigging of the two ships became entangled. A devastating broadside from Niagara raked both ships. Both Detroit and Queen Charlotte then surrendered, as did Lady Prevost and one of the schooners. The other two British ships attempted to flee but were soon also captured. Captain Oliver Hazard Perry sent a signal, announcing the victory. "We have met the enemy and they are ours," it read.

RETREAT FROM LAKE ERIE

The British naval defeat on Lake Erie was the last straw for Procter. He immediately set about organizing a full retreat up the Thames River and overland to Niagara Peninsula. On September 18, he explained the need to flee to Tecumseh and other chiefs at Fort Malden. "Listen, father!" Tecumseh pleaded. "The Americans have not yet defeated us by land…we therefore wish to remain here, and fight our enemy, should they make their appearance. If they defeat us, we will then retreat."

But Procter would not listen. Even though he had 900 troops defending the formidable Fort Malden and about 1,500 confederacy warriors in support, Procter considered the battle lost. In an attempt to maintain the alliance with Tecumseh, however, he proposed a retreat to the lower Thames. Here they would turn to fight. Reluctantly, Tecumseh and the other chiefs agreed to accompany Procter's men. About 1,200 warriors joined the march that began on September 26 after both Fort Detroit and Fort Malden were burned. Many Canadian settlers, fearing the Americans, joined the retreat. A great line of carts, wagons, cattle, and horses were soon on the move. After ten days the column reached the village of Moravian Town, about 70 miles from Detroit, and paused. Procter believed the Americans were hot on his heels. But it was only on October 2 that Major General Harrison started up the Thames with 3,500 men, including 1,500 Kentucky horsemen under Lieutenant Colonel Richard M. Johnson.

Three days later the Americans came up against Procter's defensive line deployed across a 1,000-foot-wide gap of open ground bordered on one side by the river and on the other by swamp. His redcoats stood in one continuous line while Tecumseh's warriors waited in the woods of the swamp. The 41st Regiment of Foot was dispirited, lacked faith in Procter, and had only the ammunition in their pouches. Rather than advance his infantry towards the waiting British, Harrison unleashed Johnson's Kentuckians. Galloping forward and screaming, "Remember the Raisin River," the horsemen swept through the single volley that the British were able to fire before they crashed into the line of men. Procter and his staff fled the field and the British took to their heels. Johnson wheeled his horsemen into the swamp and soon Kentuckians and Tecumseh's warriors were locked in a vicious battle. Johnson was shot five times, but somehow survived.

At first Tecumseh could be heard shouting and rallying his warriors. Then his voice was heard no more. Those warriors who saw him fall, took flight and with them went the rest of the confederacy. Moravian Town was a disastrous defeat for the British and even more so for the Indian confederacy. The British lost 28 officers and 606 men either killed or captured in exchange for only 7 American dead and 22 wounded. The Indians left only 33 dead, including Tecumseh. But his body was later recovered and removed to a secret burial place.

Accompanied by many civilians, about 400 warriors and his 246 British soldiers, Procter continued to retreat. Harrison let him go and returned to Detroit. On October 17, Harrison left for Washington. His military career was soon over. Upon reaching the British lines at Burlington Heights on Niagara Peninsula, Procter was soon ordered back to England to face court martial. For the Indian confederacy, the defeat spelled the end of hopes that they could retain control of the Ohio and Wabash valleys. Without Tecumseh, there was nobody capable of keeping all the many tribal nations aligned. Some continued to fight the Americans while others attempted neutrality.

BATTLE OF CHÂTEAUGUAY

Autumn brought 1813's most concerted effort at an American invasion of Canada. This time the operation was directed at Lower Canada, with Montreal the desired prize. It was a two-pronged plan, one against Kingston and the other using Lake Champlain as a route of approach. Both forces would link up outside Montreal to take it. The Kingston attack by a 7,300-strong force commanded by Major General James Wilkinson was intended to pin down the majority of the British forces, while Major General Wade Hampton drove up the Lake Champlain route with 5,500 men.

Wilkinson and Hampton hated each other and made no attempt to coordinate their operations. When Wilkinson fell ill, his army remained at Sackets Harbor awaiting his recovery. Hampton, finding the Lake Champlain route too difficult, shifted his army 40 miles west to follow the Châteauguay River to the St. Lawrence. Arriving at the Canadian border in late September, Hampton settled down to wait for Wilkinson's arrival. On October 18, word arrived that Wilkinson was on the march. Hampton headed for the mouth of the Châteauguay on October 21. As he crossed the border, 1,500 militiamen invoked their right to not fight outside the United States. Hampton still had 4,000 men. Facing him were 1,600 men under command of Lieutenant Colonel Charles-Michel d'Irumberry de Salaberry. His force was a mix of French-Canadian regulars known as Fencibles or Voltigeurs, militia, and native warriors. They erected a stout barricade and abattis system across a narrow front that was flanked by the river on one side and a marshy thicket on the other. De Salabarry posted 350 men behind this barrier. Behind this first position, de Salabarry established four more defensive lines. He also had troops out on either flank.

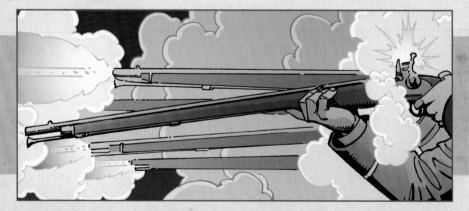

Hampton split his force in two for the attack. Colonel Robert Purdy was sent with 1,500 men to try flanking the Canadians by advancing along the river's southern bank. His main body, commanded by General George Izard, then headed for the barricade. At 2:00 in the afternoon of October 26, de Salabarry set the battle into motion by coolly raising a musket and shooting down a mounted American officer. Then, standing on a stump that exposed him to American fire, he directed his men in throwing out a steady rate of fire that drove most of the enemy to hide behind trees or logs rather than charge the outnumbered Canadians. For two hours the battle before the barricade raged while Purdy's men ineffectually tried to get behind the position on the south bank. When they finally reached a workable ford, the Americans were attacked by two companies of French-Canadian militia and a small contingent of cavalry. Purdy's men broke and ran. Seeing these troops fleeing, those in front of the barrier also withdrew. Hampton's part in the invasion of Canada was over despite his having lost only 50 men. The Canadians suffered only 5 men killed and 16 wounded. Of the battle, de Salabarry wrote, "I have won a victory mounted on a wooden horse."

CRYSLER'S FARM

Meanwhile Wilkinson, having bypassed Kingston, was advancing on Montreal with 8,000 men aboard 300 small vessels. Plagued by snowstorms and gales, the fleet struggled through the Thousand Islands until the weather cleared on November 5 and it entered the St. Lawrence River. In pursuit by boat were about 600 British regulars from Kingston commanded by Lieutenant Colonel Joseph Morrison. At Prescott, Fort Wellington blocked Wilkinson's passage. He decided to march around the fort and re-embark on the vessels, which would be floated past at night, in order to avoid a fight. This plan succeeded and the Americans were soon in sight of Long Sault Rapids, the first of a series that ran unbroken to Montreal. On the night of November 10–11, the pursuing force threatened the American rear. Morrison established his headquarters in John Crysler's farmhouse. Reinforced by local militia, some natives, and men from Fort Wellington, he had about 900 soldiers, principally the 49th and 89th regiments. Morrison also had a small number of gunboats able to bring the tail of Wilkinson's armada under fire.

From Crysler's farmhouse, a road ran virtually straight from the riverbank across an open field to Blackash Swamp, about half a mile inland. Log fences bordering the road provided stout cover for Morrison's troops. Covering his left flank in the woods beside the swamp, Morrison deployed a screen of Indians and militia. Beyond the fence line, a large wheat field gave way to a ploughed field, followed by two gullies and a ravine. Between the two gullies, a small British force composed of two companies of the 49th Regiment and three 89th Regiment companies under Lieutenant Colonel Thomas Pearson cut the road and served to funnel the Americans into fields fronting Morrison's defensive line.

Wilkinson had no choice on November 12 but to meet this threat to his rear. So he split his force, assigning 2,000 regulars under Major General John Boyd to deal with Morrison while keeping the rest with him in front of the rapids. Wilkinson was ill, bed ridden and unable to oversee the action.

Boyd advanced two brigades in three columns. The first brigade slogged across the open muddy field under rainy skies. They easily pushed in the screen of British skirmishers until the main line raked the advancing Americans with musket fire. Boyd moved the second brigade forward with one supporting cannon to reinforce the wavering first brigade. The cannon ripped holes in the British line, but it held, and both sides locked in a brisk musketry exchange.

Sensing the Americans were tiring, Morrison ordered Pearson to mount a bayonet charge against the guns. The veteran soldiers surged forward, and as the companies of the 89th fought off a cavalry attempt to block them, the 49th captured the cannon, and forced Boyd's brigades from the field. Morrison's casualties were 22 killed, 148 wounded, and 9 missing—approximately a fifth of his entire force. The Americans lost 102 killed, 237 wounded and more than 100 taken prisoner.

His line of retreat cut, Wilkinson's remaining force shot the rapids at dawn on November 13. But, learning that Hampton had retreated, he decided against proceeding to Montreal. Instead, he abandoned most of the boats and travelled cross country to the American border to take up winter quarters at French Mills on the Salmon River. This concluded American offensive action for 1813.

AMERICAN REVERSES IN THE NIAGARA PENINSULA

To bolster his Montreal invasion force, Wilkinson had stripped the American contingent on Niagara Peninsula. This allowed the British to march a small force toward Fort George, which prompted the Americans there to abandon it and retreat across the river to Fort Niagara. Before doing so on December 10, however, they evicted Newark's 400 residents and burned the town. This wanton destruction embittered Canadians, who demanded retribution.

After reoccupying Fort George, 550 British regulars led by Colonel John Murray crossed the Niagara River on December 19 and surprised the Fort Niagara garrison. The fort fell quickly with 67 Americans killed and 11 wounded, in exchange for only 5 British killed and 3 wounded. Another

344 Americans were taken prisoner and only 20 escaped. Meanwhile, another British and Indian force commanded by Major General Phineas Riall crossed the river at Five Mile Meadows and then, proceeding southwards, burned Manchester, Fort Schlosser and Buffalo. By year's end, the entire Niagara frontier on the American side was a scene of desolation.

Everyone involved in the December fighting noted the war had taken on a new shape. Scalping was common, private property looted without regard to the hardship caused civilians, buildings similarly burned. There were fewer prisoners. Soldiers, militiamen, and Indians fought to the death. The manner in which the fighting of 1813 closed portended the way of the war in the year to follow.

RUSSIAN ARBITRATION DEAD END

The failed campaign against Montreal caused consternation in Washington. President Madison, Speaker Clay, and most politicians had expected a great victory. Support for the war became shakier than ever.

International events left no reason to expect the British to incline towards negotiation. Napoleon's army had been mauled in October at Leipzig by a coalition force of Austrian, Russian, Prussian, and Swedish troops. The French lost 68,000 men over three days and were driven out of all Europe east of the Rhine. Napoleon's continental empire was finished. Tsar Alexander I had taken to the field with his army. Determined to bring Napoleon down, he had lost interest in mediating between Britain the United States.

This had been evident from the moment Albert Gallatin and James Bayard had arrived in St. Petersburg on July 21 after a long voyage. By August 1, Russian officials were warning the two men that Britain felt the Americans had too many demands and no third party could intervene successfully. If the British had no interest in a mediated settlement there was nothing Russia could do.

By now Gallatin was determined to explore every avenue to get negotiations going. He opened secret correspondence that passed through a sympathetic English banker in London to Viscount Castlereagh. While Gallatin signed his letters, Castlereagh dictated responses through the English banker, Alexander Baring. Gallatin made it clear that he, Bayard and John Quincy Adams were only

151

empowered to participate in an arbitration led by Russia. They could not directly negotiate with British representatives. After several exchanges that produced no result, Baring's response in an October 12 letter clearly confirmed that it was really Castlereagh and not the banker writing. "We wish for peace," he wrote. "The pressure of war has no object to it; it is expensive, and we want to carry our efforts elsewhere. Our desire of peace, therefore, cannot be doubted and you can rely on it." If the Americans would negotiate directly with Britain, "I think you would soon complete the work of peace without the help or hindrance of a mediator."

This was enough encouragement for Gallatin. On October 18, Gallatin sent his private secretary, George Dallas, to London to discreetly pursue how a direct negotiation could begin. With winter setting in, Russia became ice bound on November 1. Leaving by ship was no longer possible. Finally, as it was clear the Russian initiative would not proceed, Gallatin and Bayard decided to leave by horse-drawn sleigh on an overland trek to Amsterdam. From there they would either take ship back to America or be positioned to enter into negotiations with the British. The two men left at the end of January, 1814. Adams remained as America's representative to Russia.

CASTLEREAGH PROPOSES DIRECT NEGOTIATIONS

On December 30, 1813, the British schooner Bramble sailed into Annapolis under a flag of truce. Aboard was a letter from Castlereagh that reached Secretary of State James Monroe as the clock struck midnight. The British government was willing to enter into direct peace talks with the United States, Castlereagh wrote. American commissioners would be guaranteed safe passage to any destination in Europe for the talks to occur.

While President Madison and Monroe maintained the impression they were determined to continue the war, both men leapt at the offer. Monroe's reply was carried away by Bramble on January 5, 1814. "I am accordingly instructed to make known to your lordship…that the President accedes to his proposition." Two days later, Monroe reported the news to Congress and asked it to endorse John Quincy Adams, James Bayard, Henry Clay and Jonathan Russell as envoys. Albert Gallatin was added to the list on February 8. Adams was appointed chair.

Henry Clay

The appointment of the man most responsible for drawing the country into the war as a negotiator alarmed the Federalists. But Clay was presented as a counterweight to Bayard, who was considered overly pro-British. Republicans, particularly those from the American frontier, welcomed Clay's participation because they believed he would sign no treaty that failed to uphold American honour or prohibited Canada's eventual annexation. Still believing that it was the British who were stirring up the Indians, Westerners were determined that Canada must be taken.

Despite having brought about the war, Clay now equally and without apology was determined to hold centre stage in negotiating an armistice. His intention was to win through a treaty everything America had desired but been unable to achieve by war. Clay and Russell sailed for Gothenburg, Sweden on February 23. Madison thought Sweden a good location for the negotiations.

At the same time as the president dispatched his negotiation team, Madison made it clear America must continue the war. He would have preferred a defensive war. Congress made sure that was all America could wage. It rejected a call to increase the army by 55,000 men through conscription. A proposed bill to raise $45.3 million to cover naval and army costs for a year was slashed to $25 million.

BRITISH RESPONSES

Prospects for the defence of Canada had never been brighter. But Governor Prevost remained gloomy. Promised reinforcements, he countered that these would likely not arrive until the campaign season was over. His British regulars and Canadian Voltigeurs numbered about 900 officers and 15,000 other ranks. But many were sick and exhausted by the hard campaign of 1813. Even learning that Paris had fallen on March 31, followed six days later by Napoleon's abdication, failed to raise his spirits. With Europe finally at peace, the British planned to send thousands of veteran troops to Canada.

The British government also intended to settle its mastery over the Great Lakes. Vice-Admiral Sir Alexander Cochrane arrived in Halifax on April 1 and took over all naval operations in the western hemisphere. Unlike Prevost, Cochrane was offensively minded. "I have it much at heart to give them a complete drubbing before peace is made," he said of the Americans.

On April 25, he ordered the entire U.S. coastline blockaded. Suddenly British ships seemed to be everywhere along the coast. Although some of America's small warships managed to escape to sea and were successful at capturing the occasional British merchant, there was no question that the seas belonged to the Royal Navy.

Cochrane turned to the Great Lakes with similar resolve. About 250 seamen were provided to crew two new frigates, the 58-gun Prince Regent and the 43-gun Princess Charlotte, being built at Kingston. During the winter, the British had also floated the 23-gun Wolfe. Cochrane was confident these new ships in concert with five from the original fleet would be able to win Lake Ontario. Another 600 sailors and dockyard workers sent to Kingston in early spring added to British strength.

The Americans had also been busy at Sackets Harbor through the winter, but construction had been slow. By February they had just two brigs, Jefferson and Jones, near completion. Construction then began on the larger frigate, Superior. When Superior was complete, the Americans would match the British in having eight ships on the lake. But boast about 800 more sailors and a third more firepower.

SEESAW ON LAKE ONTARIO

By May the British had 1,517 men and eight ships ready. The sailors also had a willing ally in Lieutenant General Sir Gordon Drummond and a joint army-navy operation against Fort Oswego was planned. Spies reported the fort was held by only 290 regulars and the guns intended for Superior were temporarily being stored there.

On May 6, with ships shelling the fort, Drummond landed 750 redcoats, marines, and sailors. The fort fell after a sharp action but only seven long guns were found, as the rest had not yet arrived. These guns and 2,400 barrels of provisions were carried off.

Learning that the other guns for Superior had arrived at Oswego Falls, the British blockaded Sackets Harbor with five ships constantly on station to prevent their delivery. At Oswego Falls, Master Commandant Melancthon Woolsey waited with 33 cannon for an opportunity to slip in small boats past the blockade. On the night of May 28–29 he made the attempt with 19 boats. One became separated from the party, was taken by the British, and its crew betrayed the plan. An attempt to intercept the boats failed, however, and Woolsey succeeded in getting the guns through. As the guns were loaded onto Superior, the balance on Lake Ontario again came into doubt and the British had to husband their fleet to be ready for whatever campaign Prevost might have in mind.

THE AMERICAN PLAN

Not until April 30 did the Americans come up with a plan for attacking Canada. As the army could muster barely 14,000 men, Secretary of War John Armstrong proposed that Major General Jacob Brown launch an amphibious attack on Fort Erie to capture Burlington Heights and then York. This would cut the British off from the Indians to the west and isolate Niagara Peninsula.

Success depended on gaining control of Lake Ontario, so the plan was put on hold until Superior was ready. In the meantime, Brown was authorized to win a toehold on Niagara Peninsula by capturing Fort Erie and the bridge over Chippewa Creek, near Niagara Falls. Thereafter, he could seize Fort George and then march on Burlington Heights and York. Once these all fell the American campaign in the Canadas would be finished.

NEGOTIATE AND MAKE WAR

In Europe, British and American envoys were slowly moving towards negotiations. The British appointed Vice-Admiral James Gambier to lead its delegation. An expert in maritime and naval law, William Adams, also joined the commission. Although Gambier was the chair, real power lay with the third member—Colonial Office Undersecretary Henry Goulburn. All three men were under strict instruction to agree to nothing without it first being approved by Castlereagh and other senior cabinet ministers.

After much discussion, it was decided the negotiations would be held in the ancient Belgian city of Ghent. Beginning on June 24, the Americans and British started arriving. While matters of protocol and formality dominated initial discussions that began in July, the British were also preparing to send 13,000 veteran troops to Canada in a series of convoys that would see them all delivered to Quebec by year's end. The British government advised Prevost that he was to carry the war onto American soil and cease steering a purely defensive course.

CHIPPEWA

On July 3, Major General Brown crossed the Niagara with 3,400 men. Of these 2,400 were regulars divided into two brigades. The rest consisted of more than 300 artillerymen, and 600 Pennsylvania volunteers. Brown also had about 600 friendly Indians. Defending Niagara Peninsula were only 2,500 British troops scattered among several garrisons. The Americans were better trained than before due to one of the brigade commanders, Brigadier General Winfield Scott. Having been part of several previous defeats, Scott had trained the regulars hard through the winter. The result was the men were better soldiers and also had higher morale than previously.

Brown's Indians seized Fort Erie, taking its 137-man garrison prisoner. At sunrise the following day, the Americans marched from Fort Erie toward Chippewa. British scouts skirmished with the advance guard and damaged bridges to slow the Americans, but could not stop them. That evening the Americans camped on the south bank of Street's Creek and Scott decided the troops should enjoy a July 4 dinner. There was no expectation that the British would attack. Festivities were just beginning when scouts reported that the British had crossed the Chippewa River and were coming on fast.

Major General Phineas Riall had just 1,500 regulars and 300 militia and Indians under command, but he expected the usual American disorganization would result in a rapid retreat. Instead, Scott's brigade moved to meet him. Standing with backs to the river, Scott's men formed a long firing line identical to that favoured by the British. Riall's men were bunched up in column along the road. As the Americans prepared to fire, Riall shouted, "Those are regulars, by God!"

The Americans loosed a deadly volley and Riall's redcoats broke. The British lost 148 killed, 22 wounded, and 46 taken prisoner. American casualties were higher despite their advantage on the field. They had 60 killed and 240 either wounded or gone missing.

Riall withdrew to Fort George with the Americans following as far as Queenston. Here they paused on July 10 to fortify the heights. Brown was waiting on the navy to arrive with supplies and also to bombard Fort George. The American commander, Commodore Isaac Chauncey, however, had

156

lost his nerve and refused to venture from Sackets Harbor for fear of leaving it exposed to attack. Knowing the British were being reinforced daily, Brown withdrew on July 24 to the south bank of the Chippewa.

LUNDY'S LANE

On July 25, Lieutenant Colonel Thomas Pearson and a 1,000-man advance guard of British regulars set up position on top of a hill where Lundy's Lane intersected the road paralleling the Niagara River. By noon the British force had grown to 1,600 men and another 1,200 regulars and militia with two 6-pound guns were on the way from Burlington.

Brown ordered an attack, and, at about four in the afternoon, Scott's brigade approached Lundy's Lane. His force consisted of 1,072 men. A ribbon of scarlet lay unfurled across an open plain and the hill. Scott put in a hard attack that initially pushed back the British left flank. Badly wounded, Riall was taken prisoner. As twilight set in, the fighting was at close quarters all along the line. By nine o'clock Scott had only 600 men, but he had been reinforced by the entire American force. Slowly the British line began to give way until it was reinforced by the 1,200 men from Burlington.

In darkness, the fighting raged on. Cannon changed hands, men fired muskets at point-blank range. Scott was bleeding from a musket ball that shattered his left shoulder joint. Brown was shot in the right thigh and then stunned when a spent cannonball struck him. Brigadier General Eleazar Ripley took command of the Americans and ordered a retreat.

It was the war's bloodiest engagement with 171 American dead, 572 wounded, and 110 missing. British casualties numbered 84 killed, 559 wounded, 193 missing, and 42 taken prisoner. The Americans fell back to Fort Erie and braced to face a siege.

On August 1, Chauncey finally sortied from Sackets Harbor aboard Superior and blockaded the British fleet at Kingston. Declaring America now master of Lake Ontario, he spurned all criticism that it was an empty victory because the army was no longer capable of offensive action. Forced to reinforce Niagara Peninsula by overland routes rather than ships on the lake, Drummond did not feel his forces were strong enough to attack Fort Erie until the night of August 14–15. Attempting to gain surprise in the dark, the British troops became badly disorganized and the attack collapsed in disaster with 57 dead, 309 wounded, and 539 missing or taken prisoner. The Americans suffered only 84 casualties.

The siege continued through to September 21 when Drummond finally ordered a retreat to Chippewa. He was sick and so too were most of his men.

At the same time, Major General George Izard had arrived at Fort George from Lake Champlain with 3,500 men to boost the Americans to 6,300. This was the strongest and undoubtedly most efficient force the United States had yet deployed inside Canada. Izard set out on September 28 to take Fort George.

Once again Chauncey was expected to support the attack with his fleet. This expectation came to nothing, however, when the British sailed out the mighty 120-gun St. Lawrence from Kingston. Chauncey took one look and fled to Sackets Harbor, ceding control of Lake Ontario. Izard's troops straggled back to Fort Erie. On November 5, he blew up the fort and retreated across the border to Buffalo. America's last campaign against Canada was over.

WASHINGTON IN FLAMES

While the Americans had been concentrated on attacking Niagara Peninsula, Vice-Admiral Cochrane had taken the war to America with an amphibious operation into Chesapeake Bay. His objectives were no less than Washington and also Baltimore. On August 18, a large British fleet entered the bay with 4,000 regulars under command of Major General Robert Ross. Half of these men were veterans of the European war, as was Ross. Having never believed Washington or Baltimore could be seriously threatened, the Americans were caught flat-footed. On August 24, the British reached Bladensburg and were within five miles of Washington. Facing them was a line of 7,000 Americans, but only 1,000 were regulars.

The British fired a volley of Congreve rockets—iron missiles loaded with 32-pound explosive charges that spewed a stream of flame in their wake—over the heads of the Americans and the line crumbled. The British dubbed the easy win and subsequent pursuit the Bladensburg Races. Washington fell virtually without a fight.

Unlike the Americans at York, the British were under orders to burn only government buildings. Several private residences, including that of Albert Gallatin, were also burned in error. Cochrane personally wanted the office of the National Intelligencer set afire because the paper had directly scorned him in a number of issues. Beseeched by several women who feared the flames would spread to their adjacent homes, Cochrane instead ordered the building's contents ransacked and the printing press smashed. They also destroyed thousands of tons of military stores, including 200 cannon.

THE STAND AT BALTIMORE

On September 11, the British attacked Baltimore with a joint operation conducted on land and by sea. The army advancing by land was ambushed by 3,200 Americans and Ross was mortally wounded. Cochrane ordered the troops to hold in place while he attempted bombard the forts protecting Baltimore's harbour into submission. Over a twenty-four-hour period, the bombardment continued with more than 1,500 rounds being fired. Aboard a ship, American lawyer Francis Scott Key scribbled a poem while watching the shelling and observing the flag still flying over Fort McHenry even as Congreve rockets whizzed overhead and mortar bombs exploded in airbursts that spewed shrapnel into the fort. In 1931, Congress would declare the poem, "The Star Spangled Banner," America's national anthem.

Shortly after dawn on September 14, the British lifted the siege. Americans considered that Baltimore's stand offset the Washington calamity. The British deemed it a modest setback. Far graver was the Lake Champlain failure, where the British suffered a stunning defeat in the final chapter of the 1814 campaign.

PREVOST'S NERVES

In early September, Prevost set out reluctantly on an operation intended to gain entrance to the Hudson Valley and cut New England off from the rest of the United States. Along with the successes being won on the coast, this would almost certainly force New England's surrender to Britain independent of the American government. On July 11, the British had captured Eastport on Moose Island. This gave them control of Passamaquoddy Bay, quickly followed by seizing all of Maine from New Brunswick to Penobscot Bay. This positioned the British to declare that the new boundary between America and the Canadas was the Penobscot River.

Prevost was supposed to be capitalizing on these gains with an advance into the virtually unguarded Lake Champlain route. When Major General George Izard had moved 4,000 men from here to reinforce the doomed Niagara Peninsula campaign, he left behind only 3,000 regulars and militia to defend this vital gateway to New England. Brigadier General Alexander Macomb considered only

160

half of these men fit for duty. The rest were sick, raw recruits, or New York militia that Macomb didn't trust to fight.

On September 1, Prevost crossed into America with 10,000 men. Two-thirds were veterans of the Napoleon war. Prevost was anxious, considering that American control of the lake was a critical handicap. The American fleet consisted of the 26-gun flagship Saratoga, the 20-gun Eagle, a schooner, two sloops, and 12 gunboats. The British, however, were ready to challenge American dominance with a 36-gun ship captured from the French and named Confiance.

By September 5, Prevost's army was eight miles from Plattsburgh. The next day the British cautiously probed its outskirts. Unable to locate the American defences, however, Prevost did not make an all-out attack. Despite the presence of several British gunboats on the lake next to his troops, Prevost could see American ships nearby and so became increasingly cautious.

Prevost insisted on winning control of the lake before any further advance by land. Confiance was not ready for battle because its crew were soldiers being re-trained as sailors, but on September 11 an attempt was made to ambush Saratoga. The British 16-gun brig Linnet dropped anchor beside Eagle with the 11-gun Chubb supporting. The 10-gun Finch and most of the British gunboats sawed off against the 17-gun Ticonderoga and 7-gun Preble.

Confiance slammed Saratoga with a heavy broadside that killed the British commander. Finch ran aground and struck its colours while Chubb was sent drifting out of control after being smashed by fire from Eagle and soon captured.

The crew on Confiance was unable to match the seamanship of the Americans on Saratoga and soon struck its colours after being battered by repeated broadsides. Linnet also struck. The American mastery of the lake was indisputable. Having only just begun an attack on Plattsburgh when the lake battle suddenly ended, Prevost saw the surrendered or wrecked British vessels and his nerve totally failed. Prevost led his demoralized army back to Canada, crossing the border on September 14.

Whether the war continued into 1815 now rested on discussions between eight men in Ghent. These had started badly in August. Both sides came to the table demanding concessions while surrendering little themselves. The British were unwilling to abolish impressment. A declared breaking point, however, was their insistence that an Indian territory in the west be established that neither the British nor the Americans would violate by trying to purchase, conquer, or negotiate the Indians into surrendering. This would secure Upper Canada from renewed attacks by America and also bring an end to the wars between the Indians and the United States.

The Americans were horrified by the idea. They had no instructions to negotiate anything about the Indians. It was also unthinkable that the continued westward expansion of the United States could be checked. Indians were savages. They had no concept of land ownership. America's destiny lay in extending its boundaries across the continent from sea to sea. Perhaps Canada would not be part of that extension, but the rest of North America would be American. As for the Indians, they were destined to be absorbed in that expansion or eliminated.

America, the British argued, must also maintain no naval presence on the Great Lakes nor have forts along their southern shores. Those forts already existing needed to be dismantled and abandoned. The Americans could not imagine Washington accepting such a demand.

By September, both parties considered the negotiation bound to fail and were preparing to leave Ghent. Goulburn wrote to London: "I do not deem it possible to conclude a good peace now—as I cannot consider that a good peace…leaves the Indians to a dependence on the liberal policy of the United States."

In London, however, both Castlereagh and Prime Minister Liverpool were having second thoughts over the hard British negotiating line. The nation was weary after many years of war. Surely some minor concessions could be made to bring the Americans to agree to peace. At the same time, President Madison and his administration were equally desperate to end the war. But how to conclude a peace remained elusive as the talks dragged on into November.

On November 10, John Quincy Adams suddenly realized how peace could be agreed. Before the war, relations between Britain and America had been uneasy but tolerable. This was particularly so if one ignored the "outrages" of impressment and the orders-in-council. Both were no longer issues. Europe was at peace, so impressment was no longer required. And the orders had been repealed in 1812.

So why not, Adams suggested, simply "conclude the peace on the footing of the state before the war, applied to all the subjects of dispute between the two countries, leaving all the rest for future and pacific negotiations?" End the war. Then negotiate any outstanding disagreements. When the other American commissioners said they had no authority to make such a peace, Adams said it would be on his head. The proposal offered the only possible way to a treaty.

This proposal was passed to the British commissioners along with a proposed treaty that contained many items the Americans knew would be unacceptable. "We shall have no peace with America unless we acceded to their proposition of placing things…as they stood when war was declared to which I presume we are not ready to accede," Goulburn wrote to London. Goulburn was wrong. The British government was quite happy to agree to such a peace.

As November gave way to December the negotiations continued with each side quibbling over minor details. But it was clear that the intention was to finalize a treaty rather than break off discussions and continue the war into 1815. Such matters as the British possession of part of Maine and what was to become of that were set aside for later negotiation after the peace was concluded. As for the Indian confederacy and creation of a protected territory from it, the British dropped this demand. The Indians would be left to their fate. It was a bitter pill for Goulburn to swallow, for he believed it meant they would be wiped out by American expansion. They had been loyal allies and he considered the British were betraying them.

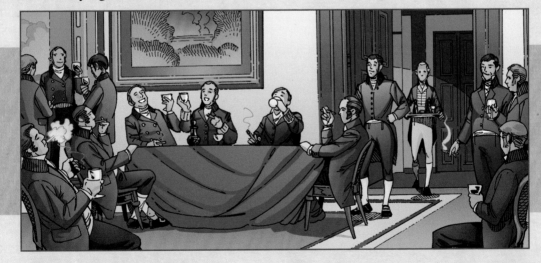

On December 24, Christmas Eve, all eight commissioners signed a treaty that effectively ended the war by returning North America to the status quo that had existed before the war. "We lose no territory, I think no honor," Henry Clay wrote. The "conditions of the peace certainly reflect no dishonor on us," the man who had pushed America into the war added in conclusion. Honour had been preserved and that sufficed.

The treaty was delivered to London within two days of their signing. But there was no rapid means of communicating news of the peace to North America. That depended on the winds that powered sailing ships across the Atlantic. To allow time for the treaty to reach Washington, its terms would stand for four months. If President Madison had not signed the treaty before that deadline elapsed, the treaty would be nullified and the war continued. Nobody in North America had the slightest idea that a peace treaty had been signed. So the war ground on with the British attacking New Orleans. Vice-Admiral Cochrane arrived off the town with 6,000 troops on December 8. Between the coast and New Orleans lay miles of swamps and bayous.

It took until January 8, 1815 for the British to work their way inland to threaten the town. The British had 4,400 men under Major General Sir Edward Pakenham while 4,500 Americans commanded by Major General Andrew Jackson faced them. The British were regulars. Jackson's force was made up of a mix of regulars, Kentucky and Tennessee volunteers, Creoles, freed slaves and a motley crew of Baratarian pirates led by Jean Lafitte.

At daybreak, the British advanced across open sugar-beet fields and came under fire from American naval guns mounted in bastions on either flank. Then the men manning cannon and muskets behind a barrier to their front opened fire. Pakenham was killed, most of the senior officers badly or mortally wounded. The British attack crumbled. It was a staggering defeat - 291 were dead, 1,262 wounded, and 484 missing. Jackson's men had lost a trifling 13 dead, 39 wounded and 19 missing.

The Americans had won a decisive victory but one that could not affect the outcome of a war already settled by treaty.

News of the victory at New Orleans reached Washington by overland courier on February 5. Nine days later a ship from Ghent arrived in New York bearing the treaty. On February 17, President Madison signed it into law. Two years and eight months after it began, the war of 1812 was at an end.

HONOUR PRESERVED

Once the war ended, the question became whether it was a good peace. Most Americans thought so. They had lost nothing. The victory at New Orleans allowed the idea to take root that America had won the war's decisive battle. That was not the case, but the myth persists. The Indian confederacy was doomed. Within three years all the continent south of the 49th parallel and east of the Mississippi, save a fragment of Spanish Florida, had been granted statehood or territorial status. Settlers, gold prospectors, buffalo hunters, fortune seekers, and freebooters of all kinds had pushed outward to the Missouri River and well beyond by the end of the decade.

The Indian nations fled before this undeclared invasion as refugees, moved to assigned reservations or faced slaughter by the army. This pattern would continue until Americans declared the west won. Only a remnant of the peoples from whom a continent was taken survived.

With territorial expansion came a massive economic boom commercially and industrially in the north and agriculturally in the southern states. The War of 1812 was seen as having provided America with a clear vision of itself as the one nation, indivisible under God that the forefathers had intended. The Civil War shattered this vision as southern and northern states fought each other in the bloodiest war in modern history from 1861 to 1865. When it was over, memory of the War of 1812 dimmed to the point that it virtually disappeared from the American conscience.

The war meant little to Britain. At first the public were horrified that it had ended without a treaty that punished America. But quickly everyone lost interest. The treaty left many issues unresolved and these took years to address through various negotiations. In 1817, the parts of Maine still claimed by the British were returned with the exception of Moose Island. Each side agreed the same year to only having a single naval ship on Lake Ontario, two on the upper lakes, and one on Lake Champlain.

Commercial agreements were gradually renewed and improved upon. The 49th parallel from Lake of the Woods to Stony Mountain was agreed as a boundary.

Public reaction to the treaty in Canada had initially been negative. Canadians looked warily at the American forts that remained on the southern shores of the Great Lakes and wondered when the next invasion would come. There was also a keen sense of wrongness about the way the Indians had been abandoned. Canada's fur trade depended on strong Indian nations and with each year that industry weakened as the American settlers pushed west, cutting down forests as they went. Although the Indians were soon being pushed back before British North America as well, there was minimal bloodshed. Disease, famine, and less-than-voluntary consignment to reserves more efficiently cleared the way at less economic cost than war.

In Upper and Lower Canada there could not be said to be a clear sense of national identity arising out of the war. But if Canadians did not yet know who they were, they knew who they were not. They were not Americans and through the war had made clear their desire to never be so. Rather than looking southward to America for inspiration, institutions, or forms of government, they looked instead across the Atlantic to Britain. This led naturally to the creation of a federal government in 1867 when the colonies confederated into the Dominion of Canada and adopted a British parliamentary model. Although most Canadians failed to recognize it at the time, the Treaty of Ghent preserved the future of what would become their nation. Combined with the new sense of selfhood fostered by the performance of the Canadian militia during the war, the conditions of the peace set British North America on the path that would in less than 50 years see the emergence of Canada as a distinct nation.

Creator Biographies

Alan Grant

Alan began his writing career in comics at DC Thomson in the 1970s, and soon moved to IPC Magazines in London where he became a regular scriptwriter on the flourishing 2000AD weekly. Amongst his many hits were STRONTIUM DOG, JUDGE DREDD and BLACK-HAWK. His work then found an international audience with DC Comics, with LOBO, BAT-MAN and THE DEMON amongst his many successes.

1991 saw the publication of the hugely-successful graphic novel Judgement On Gotham, featuring Batman and Judge Dredd. Illustrated by Simon Bisley, the book went on to break all publishing records at the time, and remains a best-seller to this day.

Alan lives in Scotland and continues to write comic books, screenplays and novels.

Claude St. Aubin

Claude St. Aubin was born in Matheson, Ontario, of French Canadian parents. He spent his teen and young adult years in Montreal, where he graduated from college as a graphic designer. He started his career as a comic book artist on the Canadian comic book CAPTAIN CANUCK. From there, he pursued a career as a graphic designer but eventually returned to his true passion as a comic book artist.

He has worked for most of the major American publishers as a freelance artist, mostly as a penciller but sometimes as an inker. He is happily married with two children and four grand children. He is still working in the comic book industry and when the opportunity arises, he works as a children's book illustrator. He is a Hall of Fame inductee and the recipient of the 2010 Joe Shuster Award for his contribution to the Canadian comic book industry.

Lovern Kindzierski

Lovern Kindzierski's colours have appeared in many comic books, magazines and animation, including ANIMAL MAN, FABLES, CORALINE, The New Yorker and Wired. He has been nominated as best colourist for the Eisner Awards, Harvey Awards, and Schuster Awards. Lovern won best colourist in the Wizard Fan Awards (twice), as well as the Comic Buyers' Guide Fan Awards. A Buyer's Guide survey named him one of the most influential colorists in the history of the industry.

Todd Klein

Todd Klein has been lettering comics since 1977. He is perhaps best known for lettering THE SANDMAN written by Neil Gaiman, nearly all of the AMERICA'S BEST COMICS line written by Alan Moore, and all of FABLES written by Bill Willingham. Todd has won sixteen Eisner Awards, eight Harvey Awards, and numerous other honors for his work. Current projects include THE UNWRITTEN, and BATWOMAN. Todd lives in rural southern New Jersey with his wife Ellen and several cats.

Mark Zuehlke

Mark Zuehlke is the author of FOR HONOUR'S SAKE: THE WAR OF 1812 AND THE BROKERING OF AN UNEASY PEACE, which won the Lela Common Canadian History Award in 2007. His award-winning and bestselling Canadian Battle Series detailing the battles and campaigns of Canada's army during World War II currently consists of nine volumes with more on the way. When complete it will be the most extensive account of any nation's battle experience during World War II ever written by a single author, which has been hailed as a major contribution to keeping the memory of Canada's war experience alive in the national conscience. Mark lives in Victoria, British Columbia.

The Loxleys and the War of 1812 School Play

Adapted from the graphic novel by Oscar nominated Hollywood screenwriter Tab Murphy, the school play presents an opportunity for students to bring history to life. Written with Grade 7 age students and above in mind, the play features the characters from the graphic novel, the Loxleys and the historical figures involved in key events from the war. It offers a great way to help students immerse themselves in this important chapter in Canadian history and also involve their local community in recreating the Canada of 200 years ago. Details are on the Renegade website.

Excerpt from the play:

Aaron sets his fiddle down and starts to walk away.

Eliza
Aaron! Where are you going?

Aaron
To pack my belongings. I'm off to fight the Americans.

Eliza
Aaron Loxley! You lost your own father in a war. Will you put your children through the same misery?

Aaron
I do not want to fight, Eliza. But sometimes a man must fight for what he believes in. I believe in this family. And I believe in this land. And that is why I must go.

Matthew
It is absurd! How can you even think of fighting our neighbors across the Niagara? We trade with them each week. They are our friends!

William
Is Matthew not right, father? What difference does it make whether we are ruled by a King or a President? We farm the land, whoever rules us.

Aaron
The land we farm is our land. Canadian land. The Americans want to take it. And we cannot allow them.

The Loxleys and the War of 1812 novel
by Alan Grant

Written with those who want to immerse themselves deeper into the world of the Loxleys in mind, Alan's novelisation takes us into the heart of their lives, emotions and actions. With chapter illustrations from two of Canada's bright young artists, Alexander Vincent and Meagan Hotz, this book is a great fireside read.

Excerpt from the novel:

He walked a little way upstream and saw a fallen log that bridged the ravine, spray rising from the rapids below it. This would be his crossing point. Holding his arms wide for balance, taking a deep breath, George began to walk across the slippery log.
Halfway across, his foot slipped on the damp wood and he started to fall. He reached desperately to clutch onto a stump of branch that protruded from the log and hung there precariously,

"Help!" he cried out, even though he knew there would be no-one around who could save him. "Somebody help me!"

A short distance away, a large buck rabbit paused as it nibbled at the long grass. The animal pricked up its ears and, startled by the unaccustomed human voice, darted back into the cover of the forest.
A fraction of a second after the rabbit had moved, an arrow thudded into the tree trunk behind where it had stood.
There was a soft curse and an Indian boy stepped out from his hiding place. He held a bow in one hand and a quiver of arrows was strapped across his back. He wore a loose, beaded buckskin tunic, with one dead rabbit already slung from the belt that held up his buckskin trews. Sturdy moccasins adorned his feet.

"Help!"

The boy paused as he heard the faint cry and altered direction to take him towards the gorge from which it came. Moments later he stood on the edge of the ravine, staring hard at the figure dangling from a fallen log. The figure had seen him, too, and even as the Indian turned to leave, it redoubled its pleas for help.
"Please - do not go. I cannot hold on much longer..."
Conflicting emotions tore through the Indian boy's mind. He was not one to leave a fellow being in trouble, and yet...

The War of 1812 Timeline

www.1812timeline.com is our website that takes you through the events leading up to, during and after the war with links to good historical resources and current events planned for the bicentenary.

The timeline also incorporates the characters from our graphic novel into the actual historical events, as well as allowing event organisers to add their 1812 bicentenary event to the current event timeline to help spread the word and raise awareness.

Scan this QR code to visit the timeline:

Or type www.1812timeline.com into your web browser.

Initial Character Designs
by Claude St. Aubin

The Loxleys

Rebecca   Ellen   Aurora   Eliza   Verity

Tecumseh and Firebrand

Aaron

William

Matthew

George

Pierre

175

Claude St. Aubin